Pushing Up Daisy

A Josephine Stuart Mystery

by

Joyce Oroz

For information, email **Cozy Cat Press**, cozycatpress@aol.com or visit our website at: www.cozycatpress.com

COZY CAT
PRESS

ISBN: 978-1-946063-36-6

Printed in the United States of America

Cover design by Paula Ellenberger
www.paulaellenberger.com

1 2 3 4 5 6 7 8 9 10

I am dedicating this book to my daughter, Cindy Laurin, because she gave me the idea and a nudge to write about Park Theater and the wonderful children who perform there. "Pushing Up Daisy" was a lot of fun to write. In my mind, I lived in the little town of Ben Lomond for the nine months it took to complete the story.

Many thanks to my editor and dear friend, Tomiko Edmiston, for her sharp eye, good instincts and great suggestions.

Sincere thanks to my husband, Arthur Oroz, who keeps me on track—in the real world as my "realty-police." A big thank you goes to Kate and Janinne for inspiring me with their wonderful, imaginative productions at Park Theater, year after year.

And, as always, thanks to Patricia and Cozy Cat Press for publishing my stories.

Chapter 1

A ten p.m. call from Aunt Clara and a ten-thirty call from Clara's friend, Kate, had convinced me I should paint props for the Little People's Repertory Theater, located in Park Theater, Ben Lomond, California. Not only was I roped into a pro-bono prop-painting position, but Kate asked me to recruit my two talented mural-painter employees, Alicia Quintana and Kyle Larson. I wondered if they would be willing to donate their time.

Over the phone, Kate told me about Mac, the set-painter. She said he was a legend. He showed up Friday morning, the first day of stage-preparation for a new play, measured walls, conferred with Kate and Janinne, and sketched out some of the scenery with chalk. He had worked hard for several hours, but no one remembers seeing him after the lunch break. Mac was not seen again until Saturday evening when an electrician found him in the theater's attic, released from the physical world, staring blankly at one-hundred-year-old redwood rafters.

I confessed to Kate that I would be available for the next three weeks because my "mural on the mall" project had hit a wall of red tape, which meant that Alicia and Kyle would also be available. As we talked, I realized that public exposure at the theater might bring attention to my Wildbrush Murals Company, thereby shedding a good light on a contract with the city. Although I had never met Kate in person, I did know that her mother happened to be on the Santa Cruz City

Council and was influential when it came to art on the mall.

I punched in Alicia's number.

Alicia yawned before she spoke. "Jo, don't you think it's a little early to be calling…?"

"Sorry. I know Sunday mornings are sacred, but this is important. Remember when I told you about Aunt Clara working with kids at the Park Theater, helping them with their lines and costumes? Well, she called late last night to give me a heads up. She told me there had been some serious trouble at the theater and that her friend Kate was looking for people to paint sets. A few minutes later, Kate called to tell me their head painter died."

"Was he real old?"

"No, she said Mac was a high school teacher and every summer he volunteered to paint the scenery for the theater production. It seems he was multi-talented. He played in the orchestra for all nine performances every summer. Kate said his drums would drown out some of the player's lines, but he played for free."

"So how did he die?" Alicia asked, sounding wide-awake.

"They found him in the theater's attic. The day he painted, it was a hundred and four outside, but much hotter in the attic."

"Eww! How awful," she groaned.

"I know, and Kate said the door was locked. I guess you'll have to skip church today…."

"Jo, are you saying we go to work today?"

"That's what I'm asking you to do. It'll be fun. Wear shorts and bring water. I'll pick you up at eleven. Gotta call Kyle now…bye."

***

Alicia was easy compared to Kyle who sounded like he had been out celebrating all night, not unusual for a lanky redheaded college student with a shy smile and a steady girlfriend. With my usual finesse, I talked him into meeting us at the theater in Ben Lomond at noon, giving him a few hours to get his earring collection in order.

Speaking of getting stuff in order, I gathered up a handful of my favorite paint brushes, a three-foot ladder and my handy two-foot measuring level, placed everything in the bed of my Mazda pickup truck and pulled the "snug-top" down. Working as a professional muralist, these items were invaluable to me.

After my uninsured husband, Marty, died seventeen years ago under an eighteen-wheeler, I began painting murals for a living. A couple of years ago, I hired Alicia and Kyle to help with the workload. Success for me looked like a little adobe house on five grassy acres in the tiny town of Aromas, California, where my sweet basset, Solow, welcomed me home and my fiancé, David Galaz, lived right next door.

Part of me wanted to stay home enjoying mild temperatures once the fog lifted and a cool evening when the fog returned. June and July in Ben Lomond would be a whole different story. Forty miles away with the wooded mountains surrounding it, the little town sizzled in the summer, creating wonderful conditions for swimming in the San Lorenzo River—but we weren't going swimming. We were going to paint sets in a big old theater with a front door, a side door and tiny windows. I found out later that the air conditioner (such as it was) was only used when the place was packed with people, nine performances for two weeks in July.

If there had been room in my truck, I would have taken Solow with me, but having Alicia in the passenger seat would be fun too. We hadn't seen each other since our last day of work four days ago so, of course, we would have plenty to talk about.

The Quintanas usually invited me over for dinner Friday nights, but this week they went to Trigger's soccer match and later, a family dinner with Ernie's mother. I adored the handsome little ten-year-old and had attended many of his soccer and baseball games.

As I packed my lunch, filled Solow's water bowl and prepared to leave the house, I felt my heart skip a beat. I figured it was the usual "new job jitters," fear of the unknown and all that rot. It happened the first day of every mural job and seemed to be happening with painting theater props as well. But even more than the excitement of a new type of painting, in a new location, with a whole new set of people, was the unsettling possibility that Mac might have been murdered. After all, Kate said the door was locked from the outside!

Solow knew I was about to leave and pressed his body against my calves.

There was a quick tap on the back door and a second later, David walked into the kitchen looking ruggedly handsome in his faded Levis and denim shirt. His thick salt and pepper hair was a bit tussled, and he smelled delicious like only David could.

"Hey, Josie, where are you going dressed in paint clothes on a Sunday?" His dark chocolate eyes searched my green ones.

I flicked my shoulder length auburn hair back and smiled. "I'm going to Ben Lomond to paint sets at the theater because the head painter died… actually he was sort of murdered."

"Murdered? Oh boy, here we go again."

"I'm just going to help with the painting, that's all. Alicia and Kyle are helping out too. It won't be bad, just four days a week for three weeks. They're really in a pinch."

"And you haven't given the murder a second thought?"

"That's right." I blushed.

He laughed. "Do you mind if I cut the grass while you're gone?"

"Of course not, just don't roll that machine of yours," I said over my shoulder as I shoved breakfast dishes into the dishwasher. I worried about David riding his tractor-mower up and down the hills, even though he had been mowing the grass for years without incident.

With kitchen cleanup finished, I slung my purse over my shoulder, walked to the front door and said goodbye to David with a kiss and to Solow with a pat on his pointy head. I backed my little red pickup down the long gravel driveway onto Otis. Two miles later, I was roaring through the world's salad bowl on San Juan Road, lettuce fields to the left, berries to the right as far as I could see.

Coastal fog lifted as I approached Alicia's neighborhood in Watsonville. She lived ten miles northwest of Aromas in a two-story house at the edge of Drew Lake. I curbed the truck in front of her place where she stood waiting, looking like a thirty-five-year-old Hispanic beauty wishing she had Sunday off to be with her family. But her smile had only diminished temporarily. Drama was not her "thing." She was my down-to-earth friend who had righted my ship many times.

Ten-year-old Trigger waved from a second floor window. I waved back. His sweet Grandma Quintana stood beside him waving.

Traffic on Highway One going north was slow, mainly because it was the end of June, kids were out of school, and Santa Cruz beaches beckoned. Alicia had questions. I had very few answers. I only knew what

Kate had told me—that we would paint every Friday, Saturday, Sunday and Monday for three weeks in a row.

My biggest concern was the rough commute, driving in heavy traffic from one end of Santa Cruz County to the other. But because I had never painted sets before, the painting challenge intrigued me and kept the other half of my brain busy speculating.

In my seventeen-year-long mural-painting career, I had never turned down a job nor ever said, "Sorry, I can't do that." I always told my clients not to worry, "I can do that." And then I would go home and figure out how "I could do that." It might mean using a new type of paint or a taller ladder or researching the color of a wallaby or the shape of a goldfish, but everything so far had been doable.

"Jo, are you thinking about the so-called murder?"

"That's the last thing on my mind…."

"Yeah, and my name is Lola from Capitola. What does David think about it?"

"He's skeptical, like you. Between you two and my mother, there isn't much I can do."

Alicia laughed, "We'll see about that."

We drove the curvy two-lane Highway Nine as it cut through a dense forest of pervasive redwood trees in the San Lorenzo Valley. Leaving Santa Cruz, Scotts Valley and Felton in the rear view mirror, we ended our trip in Ben Lomond with a left turn onto Mill Street at the only signal light in town. One block down the street, I pulled my truck to a stop in front of a two-story white stucco structure boasting five decorative windows, two with shutters and flower boxes. An overall geometric design of brown beams and boards decorated the walls, capped off with a pointy Swiss chalet-type roof.

"Here we are. Cute, isn't it?" I said as we climbed out of our seats.

Aunt Clara had told me the history of the building. Originally it had served the community as a stable and blacksmith shop. Later it housed the town's one and only water-pumper fire-vehicle. At some point, a ticket window and stage were added, turning the place into a theater. From the street, the building's footprint covered half a block.

Alicia and I walked through an entrance alcove on the West side of the building, opened one of the double doors next to a ticket window and entered a cavernous interior featuring up-to-date lighting overhead. I noticed window seats upstairs for the light, sound and special effects technicians. Dozens of metal light fixtures hung from the high ceiling, pointing this way and that, but all in the general direction of an imposing multi-level stage at the opposite end of the room.

Our hollow footsteps tapping the empty hardwood floor announced us.

Off to our right stood a young woman bent over a cardboard and paper project laid out across a long folding table. A baby strapped to her chest watched us as we came closer. The mother looked up, rounded the table and greeted us with, "You must be Josephine." She wiped glue off her hands with a wet cloth. "I'm Kate and this little gal is Gypsy."

She smiled and we shook hands.

Gypsy hiccupped.

"This is Alicia Quintana, one of my assistants."

The entrance door creaked and heavy boots came closer.

I looked over my shoulder. "And here comes Kyle."

Alicia turned and snagged Kyle's arm. "And he's the best artist at UCSC, ask anyone."

Kyle's ears reddened, as he pulled off his yellow helmet and black leather chaps.

"Thanks, you guys, for coming on such short notice. Theater work is time-sensitive. We have three weeks to put this puppy together." Kate flipped brunette bangs out of her eyes, stepped closer to the table project and pointed to a cardboard box big enough to house a large microwave oven. The top and front of the box had been cut away. Inside was a handmade poster board replica of the stage area, all tricked out with scenery and a pirate ship.

"Very impressive," I belted out over a loud grinding noise coming through the open side door.

Alicia bent down for a closer look at the box, letting a long complimentary "ahh" float off her tongue.

"What's all that noise outside?" I asked Kate.

"Carpenters," she shouted over the sawing, drilling and hammering. "In this model you'll notice that we have various props that will be recreated on a large scale out of wood. The carpenters are cutting the pieces as we speak." Kate pointed back to the box. "And there will be a staircase here and balconies there and there," pointing to the right and left sides of the stage area.

"And what are these?" Kyle asked.

"My rough impression of rocks, mermaids on the rocks, a sailing ship, and a bunch of little boy pirates climbing trees," Kate laughed.

Kyle fluffed Gypsy's dark hair with two long fingers. "Wait till the kid is about six years old—you'll know all about kids climbing trees."

"Kate, what a darling bear…." Alicia said.

"That's Baloo from Jungle Book."

Gypsy cooed, "Bah..loo..loo..looo."

"And the design on the back wall?" I asked.

"Hamilton," she said as she adjusted the strap on Gypsy's sling. "Janinne, our writer, incorporates two or three themes into every script—every year. Even the old songs are tweaked with new words to go with the play. We have sell-out crowds every performance—every year."

Gypsy clapped her hands. Maybe it was patty cake. "Bah…looooo."

Kate motioned for us to follow her. We climbed a long steep staircase, walked through a small office and entered a high-tech lighting and sound room. In front of a panel of electronics was a long window facing the stage area, at least sixty feet away.

Next, we clunk, clunked back down the stairs, crossed the open hardwood floor and climbed five short steps up to the stage. Every wall had been painted flat black, like clean chalkboards ready for the next creation. Kate pointed to balconies on each side and various areas where we would be painting. About six weeks later, all our work would be painted over with black paint, making the stage ready for a new play production.

Gypsy mimicked her mother by pointing one chubby finger around the room.

Next, Kate took us through a doorway at the right side of the stage to a back room and behind that, a long hallway running the length of the building. At one end, an old sink caught the drips from paint brushes dangling from a shelf above. Pint, quart and gallon-size cans of paint sat shoulder-to-shoulder on shelves stretching the length of the back wall. Kate mentioned that all the paint had been donated.

Kate didn't offer to take us up to the attic, the notorious room looming to our left. Yellow tape had been stretched across the bottom stair rails. I looked up at a dozen or so wooden steps and two lengths of wood railing running at a steep angle up to a modest landing in front of an elderly door that had shed most of its white paint. The rusty latch looked ancient, sad and ashamed like the door it was attached to.

That was the moment I made up my mind to visit the attic at my first opportunity.

Chapter 2

From the tenth step of a twelve-foot ladder, I heard a familiar voice and one clipped bark that sounded like, “Hello.” Carefully twisting my body, I cranked my head around. Yep, it was Aunt Clara, fluffy white hair, colorful muumuu billowing and flip flops flapping, accompanied by a sleek black and mahogany Rottweiler with a tie-dye scarf around her thick neck. Sara galloped across the wood floor, leaving Clara to catch up. The giant she-dog looked scary at first glance, but her big brown eyes and sweet ways quickly convinced my painters that she was not a threat. In reality, she was a beautiful rescue from Bakersfield, abandoned and eventually adopted by my Auntie and her new husband, Ben.

Aunt Clara introduced Sara to Alicia and Kyle, who had cautiously climbed down their ladders. Sara moved in a tight circle, giving each painter equal opportunity to pet her. When I rubbed her ears, she sniffed me and turned her head as if looking for Solow. Even though they had only met once, I knew she loved him, and Solow had been enamored with Sara, but his short legs had prevented him from expressing his obvious intentions.

“You people are fast,” Clara’s voice echoed across the theater. “What’s that thing you’re drawing, Kyle?”

“It’s going to be an old sailing ship out on the bay.”

“Yes, I see….”

Gypsy waved her chubby arms and squealed as Sara pranced in the glow of painter adoration.

"Does Sara like the baby?" Alicia asked.

"Do kittens like milk? Of course, Sara loves Gypsy," Clara said.

Kate nodded as she unwrapped her baby girl and sat her down on the floor in an out-of-the-way spot near the doors to the closets where giant stacks of folding chairs were stored.

Sara trotted over, sniffed Gypsy and lay down beside her. From that moment on, wherever Gypsy was, Sara was close by. Clara said that was the way it had been since they first met. The only thing that had changed was the baby's ability to scoot around. She didn't crawl. She scooted around on her tush and was getting better at it everyday. Sara constantly repositioned her large body against Gypsy, making sure the baby didn't go far.

My painters and I scurried back up our ladders. Using chalk and reference pictures, we continued what Mac had started two days ago. Using my level, I sketched a very ornate top railing of the ship, and Alicia and Kyle drew portholes and a door with a winged skeleton decoration above it.

Using two fifteen-foot ladders to reach the highest spots on the back wall, Alicia and Kyle measured and taped a grid across and up and down. I helped with the lower sections. That design was the "Hamilton" part of the play.

Each time I climbed down the ladder and moved it over, I looked behind me across the theater to see what Sara and Gypsy were doing. As I glanced across the room, I saw a mom and her three kids walk into the building. Clara had to coax the children away from Sara long enough to get their names and measurements written down. The mom inspected fabric samples for costumes as other moms and kids arrived and lined up to be measured.

By two o'clock, the theater felt like it was running a temperature. Everyone wore a red face and sucked on bottled water. Our measuring and drawing continued for another hour. Just when I thought I might come down with heatstroke, Kate came up to me and asked if we painters would like to take a break across the street in the park. She said the owner of the Ben Lomond Market next door had donated a cold watermelon and several "Mountain Man" sandwiches for us to enjoy.

Enjoy we did, under giant redwoods, sitting at a long picnic table listening to gentle gurgles and splashes from the shallow waters of the San Lorenzo River fifty yards and a wire fence away. In the winter months, it would become a torrent of deep, fast-moving water. For many years, the river had been dammed up each summer for recreational purposes and disassembled in the autumn before the winter rains. Swimming ended when the dam permanently disappeared, then the fish were free to spawn and children found refuge in their phones and computers.

Fortunately, the Little People's Repertory Theater provided plenty of summer fun, instruction and opportunity each year to over seventy children between the ages of eight and fourteen. My Aunt Clara never had children of her own and loved working with the young actors. Her sewing ability and grandma attitude made her a favorite with the kids.

"Isn't that the new girl...Tabatha, over there trying to climb the fence?" Clara asked, swatting at a buzzing yellow jacket attacking her roast beef sandwich.

Kate nodded as she gave Gypsy another bite of her sandwich. "Tabatha comes around everyday, looking bored. We should find a job for her."

"I wonder if she can sew," Aunt Clara said.

Gypsy spit out a piece of lettuce and flapped her arms like a chickadee.

"I think she said she's fourteen," Kate said. "She only has this one chance to be in the play. Next year she'll be too old. I'm hoping an opening comes up, but our list of children wanting to be in the play is way longer than the number we need—or can handle."

The next time I looked for Tabatha at the fence, she was gone. For one second I wondered if she had actually climbed the chain-link fence.

"Kate, that was a great lunch," I said. "I'm going down to look at the river."

Alicia and Kyle followed me to the fence that was perched at least twenty feet above the river. We stood staring into lazy water at the bottom of the ravine, scheduled to fill up rapidly during the winter months. The San Lorenzo Valley had been deluged with 124 inches of rainwater in 1889, but for over a century the typical amount clocked in at between forty and eighty inches a year. No wonder the redwood trees were so big and lived so long.

"Isn't that Tabatha down there?" Alicia pointed down river about a hundred yards to a teenager making her way south, splashing and swinging her arms, sometimes hopping from rock to rock.

"Yep, I remember she was wearing a purple tank top and white shorts," I said. "I wonder how she got down there." I scanned the length of fence encircling the block-long park, all the way back to our table where Aunt Clara bounced Gypsy on her knee and Sara sat at attention obviously wishing for a turn.

I turned my head for one last look at Tabatha as she sloshed down-river without a care in the world it seemed. She carried her flip flops in one hand, her long brown hair swaying side to side.

A well-built young man wearing jeans, a tight black t-shirt and tennis shoes emerged from the heavily wooded hillside opposite us, entered the water and followed Tabatha's steps from a hundred feet behind.

"Jo, come on," Kyle said. "Like, what's the matter?"

"Nothing, I just need to ask Tabatha something."

"But she's way down there…" he pointed, as I raced past him up to the picnic table and without stopping, onto the sidewalk. After one and a half blocks of pounding concrete, my mature fifty-year-old body jiggling from head to toe, I came to the main intersection of Ben Lomond, consisting of a four-way stoplight and a bridge over the river. The light was red. My imagination ran amok. Finally, the light went green, I ran across the street, veered off the side of the road and down a steep dirt path that curved to the right and ended at the water's edge.

Standing on a sandy beach partially shaded by the bridge, I looked up and down the river. Lovely ripples sparkled in the sun as nature's gift of life flowed toward Santa Cruz and the Pacific Ocean. Listening to the gurgling water and the occasional vehicle rumbling overhead, I almost forgot my concerns for Tabatha.

A rustle behind me chilled my blood. I twirled around and looked up the sandy bank to the underbelly of the bridge. Two teens sat on a log eating candy bars. I walked closer.

"Hi, I'm Josephine…I saw you in the theater today."

"Yeah, I saw you too. I'm Tab and this is my brother, Al."

Standing near them, it was easy to see the resemblance—dark eyes, pale skin and thick brown hair. They looked at each other as if to ask what I was doing in their private space.

"I've heard so much about Mac and what a great painter, musician and teacher he was…I was just wondering if you knew him…."

Al looked away.

Tabatha answered, "He was our uncle and we had just moved in with him and Aunt Daisy. Like, we have to be going because my aunt will be waiting for us." She stood up, popped the last bite of candy into her mouth and trotted down to the river.

Al caught up to his sister and splashed along the river's edge. They disappeared around the bend.

As I turned to leave, I saw a cell phone half buried in the sand near the log where Albert and Tabatha had been sitting. I held it in my hand for a few minutes thinking the kids would miss it and come back, but no one came back so I put the phone in my pocket and retraced my steps. Hoofing it back down the sidewalk toward the park, I told myself the cell phone was private property, but I didn't actually listen to myself or to that kind of mental nonsense. When it came to solving a murder and bringing about justice, my rule was: anything goes.

Before entering the park, I pulled the phone out of my pocket and poked at it, fumbling my way to Tabatha's email account. The cell phone pixies were with me. A list of contacts popped up. I scrolled down the list, recognizing five names: Albert, Mac, Daisy, Janinne and Kate.

I caught up to my painters as they crossed the street and entered the hot stuffy theater. Clara, Sara and Kate were right behind us, Gypsy strapped to her mother's back as usual. Someone tapped me on my shoulder. I whirled around.

"Tabatha…ah…."

"Josephine, did you happen to see a cell phone?"

"As a matter of fact I did." I pulled the phone out of my pocket and handed it to her. "Do you know anything about painting, Tabatha?"

"I took a class in painting, but I'm not very good at it. Singing is what I love to do. Do you need help with anything else? I used to like to draw…because my brother liked to draw. We did everything together until, ah….we moved to Ben Lomond."

"That's okay, Tab. I think we have it covered. You might want to ask Kate about being in the play."

Tabatha turned her head and looked nervously over her shoulder as one of the carpenters entered through the side door carrying a piece of cut wood for a ramp he was building, a ramp leading from the main floor up to the front of the stage.

Alicia and Kyle climbed their ladders and began drawing on the black walls with white chalk.

I had just placed my foot on the first rung of my ladder when Tabatha tapped my shoulder and whispered for me to follow her to the back room.

"What's going on, Tab?"

"Shhh…" she put a finger to her mouth and looked over her shoulder.

I left my sketches and chalk on the floor and followed Tabatha around the corner to the back room, past the old paint-spattered sink and rows of paint cans rusting on four long shelves. An old bare wooden bench butted up against the staircase to the attic where yellow plastic tape drooped.

Tabatha sat down on the bench.

I followed her lead.

"Josephine, I've been talking to your Aunt Clara. She says you have a real talent for catching murderers. Al and I need your help. We can pay you…really we can. You see Albert was just hired at the Ben Lomond Market for the summer. He'll be stocking shelves…."

"Tab, I'm not a pro at this sort of thing, but sometimes I get lucky. I would never charge money for solving a murder, but if I can help you, I certainly will. You first need to put your faith in the police…let them do their job…."

"They won't be much help." Her voice slipped down to a whisper.

"Why not?"

"I already told them what I know and they acted like I was just a kid. Okay, maybe I am a kid, but I know what I saw."

Chapter 3

Sunday felt like it would never end. Alicia, Kyle and I worked up a sweat drawing twisted trees, a lagoon in the distance and giant rock formations on the walls of the Ben Lomond Theater.

Around four o'clock Aunt Clara said she had to head for home, but before she left she invited all of us to dinner at her place in Boulder Creek, just fifteen miles from the theater.

"Like, I'm meeting up with someone at six," Kyle said, his face in a full blush.

Alicia raised her eyebrows a couple of times and smiled.

"I don't need to be anywhere," she said. "Ernie and Trigger are going to a ball game this evening. How about you, Jo?"

"Well, David's home but we hadn't planned anything. I'll call him and ask him to feed Solow."

Clara looked pleased. She turned and walked to the front door with Sara. I had spent a lot of time with David lately. I was spoiled having him right next door, always helping me with chores. Maybe an evening away would be good for both of us.

We three painters collapsed our ladders and left Ben Lomond to the natives. Kyle headed back to Santa Cruz on his yellow Honda motorcycle, and I drove Alicia north toward Boulder Creek. I thought about what Tabatha had told me. Should I share it with Alicia? Of course I should. She was my best friend.

"Allie, are you asleep?"

Alicia opened her eyes and straightened her sitting position.

"I was just resting my eyes and thinking about warts."

"Warts?"

"Trigger has several little warts on his left hand. Do you know anything about warts?"

"No, not really," I said. "I talked to Tabatha today. She told me things about Mac and his wife and some other people…."

"That's nice…."

"She has some ideas about the murder."

"Who says it was murder?" Alicia smirked.

"The latch was down. There's no way Mac could have locked the door; he was inside and the lock was outside…."

"Maybe someone locked the door not knowing anyone was inside." Alicia stared out the window where an endless line of redwood trees whipped by. The road curved right and left all the way to Boulder Creek, straightening as it cut through the historic mountain town, then went all curvy again up the Big Basin Highway.

"Tabatha told me that she and her brother had walked to town the evening Mac died. They stopped at the market to buy sodas. When they came out of the store and walked further down the sidewalk toward the theater to see if their uncle was there, a very tall barefoot guy was in the alley between the store and the theater. She said this stranger saw them and ducked back into the shadows behind a shed where all the stage building supplies are kept."

"Sounds a bit suspicious, but it could have been anyone—for any reason," Alicia muttered.

"Tabatha said they pounded on the front door and looked all around the building for Mac. They finally gave up; but as they were leaving, Tab looked up into this big old pine tree growing behind a shed located in the alley and there was the barefoot guy—way up in the tree, crouched on a branch being real quiet."

"Odd, but not illegal."

"Yeah, that's what the police thought when she told them. Hang on, Allie, this is Tinker Ranch Road." I cranked the wheel to the left and we careened across the two-lane highway and up a one-lane paved road, then onto a gravel extension for another mile. I braked the truck as we approached a private property sign beside a metal gate at the edge of a meadow the size of two football fields.

Alicia jumped out of the truck and slid the gate to one side along a metal track. We bumped over the track and headed west, into the setting sun.

"Sure is pretty up here," Alicia said, as she admired range after range of wooded mountains surrounding the meadow full of wildflowers and one lovely weeping willow.

"Wait till you see the view from Aunt Clara's house." *Rather cabin,* I thought to myself, remembering the hundred-year-old no-frills structure with its own outdoor wooden porta-potty featuring a half moon carved into the door.

We rolled by a giant barn painted dark green, an old tractor and an apple orchard. I pushed down the gas pedal as we started up a steep hill, the last quarter mile of the trip. The hill crested and we sidled up to Ben's white pickup truck.

Something was different. The outhouse was missing. No sad thoughts about that, I smiled.

"What's so funny, Jo?"

"I'm just impressed with the beautiful new flower gardens. Somebody's been busy. It looks like Aunt Clara's touch, except for the fancy brickwork and snazzy new barbecue." My gaze went back to the house when I heard Sara bark. She burst out the door and ran toward us.

Alicia cringed.

"Don't worry, Allie; she loves everyone." By that time, Sara was leaning her massive sleek body against us, hinting for a good rubbing. We loved her up until Clara came bustling out the door, white hair billowing, and hugged Alicia and then me.

"You've really done nice things to the place," I said.

"We work well together. Ben's making dinner right now," she said, smiling into the bright sunset sky with a hand shielding her eyes.

My first thought was, knowing Ben, we'll be having beans. But as we stepped into the kitchen, there was Ben chopping salad ingredients. A new woodblock island had been added to the extra-large country kitchen. Chopped yellow peppers, red onion, mushrooms and beets were ready to be added to a large bowl of baby greens.

"Hi, Ben; it smells delicious in here," I said, staring at the oven.

He wiped his hands on the dishtowel tied around his waist, and gave each of us a warm hug.

"Is that apple pie I smell?" Alicia asked.

Ben nodded. "My mom's recipe…hope you like it. Excuse me, gotta turn the ribs." He darted out the door.

Clara laughed. "He's in love with his new barbecue."

I remembered a big pot of beans simmering atop a very old wood-burning stove the last time I was in the old homestead. The stove had been upgraded to a stainless steel commercial stove with double ovens. The original enamel kitchen sink had been replaced with double stainless steel sinks encased in wall-to-wall granite countertops. But the same old clock on the wall ticked away as if nothing had changed.

"Anything we can do to help?" Alicia asked.

"Thank you, dear, but you girls have been on your feet all day. Have a seat." She pointed to the kitchen table with six straight-back wooden chairs from George Washington's time, possibly.

We sat down.

"Was everything okay today, I mean with Tabatha?" Clara asked.

"Yeah, at first I thought some guy was following her, but he turned out to be her brother. I was glad I had a chance to talk to her. She said Mac was her uncle. I didn't know what to say to her."

"Don't worry about it. I don't think she got along with him, and I'm sure that Albert didn't. Tabatha and Albert have only been in town for a week and already they're the talk of the town."

"What do you mean by that, Auntie?"

"A few days ago Mac was explaining to his student painters how the props should be painted. Suddenly Albert fell off a ladder he was not supposed to be sitting on while plugged into his music. It was a short ladder and Al wasn't hurt, but Mac's face turned red. He collected himself, told Al to go home and pointed to the door. It was a very uncomfortable moment for all of us volunteers. Mac never had kids of his own, and even though he taught English at the high school, I don't think he cared much for teenagers."

"Maybe he didn't like Albert for some reason," Alicia said.

"I guess that's possible, but I think Al's a very nice boy from everything I've seen. He's always looking after his sister."

Clara swabbed the counter top with a sponge where Ben had been stirring up a homemade honey-mustard salad dressing. They worked as a team, Ben making messes and Aunt Clara cleaning them up. Clara never met a food she couldn't burn but she had an instinct for tidying up a kitchen. Ben was a bit messy when cooking, but we discovered that he could whip up a fabulous meal.

Later in the evening, after a fat serving of apple pie a la mode, I was ready to head home. Alicia looked as tired as I felt. We thanked our hosts and fastened our seat belts for a ride back to Watsonville and Aromas. After a few miles of quiet digesting, we began to talk—mainly Alicia keeping me awake with her chatter.

"Jo, don't worry about me driving myself to the theater from now on. I'm going to bring Trigger with me tomorrow and give his grandmother a rest. Your Aunt Clara sure looked happy when you agreed to stay at their house on work nights. Will you have Solow with you?"

"Yep, he'll be fine with all the kids and Sara and everyone. Actually, he'll probably sleep through most of it. I think we're off to a good start, work wise."

"I think so too," Alicia said. "And we have every Tuesday, Wednesday and Thursday off. Did Kyle tell you that he's working for one of his professors, and he only has weekends to work at the theater?"

"He told me, and I think it'll be fine. I think we'll finish on time. Here we are…."

"Home already," Alicia yawned. "See you tomorrow." She slammed the passenger door and waved goodbye.

Golden light flooded the Quintana's porch. The front door opened and Ernie stepped out. He waved to me.

My porch light was also lit, thanks to David's thoughtfulness.

Solow gave me a warm welcome and David asked a ton of questions, like, how was work, did you enjoy it and who do you think murdered Mac?

"How would I know who murdered Mac?"

"If you don't know now, you will later. I know you, Josie…."

"Maybe I'm not even looking into it…."

"And my name is Pope David," he snorted.

"All I know so far is that Tabatha and Albert moved in with their Aunt Daisy and Uncle Mac…."

"Hey, did Mac teach English and music?"

"Yeah, how did you know?"

"I used to play golf with a guy named Mac and I'm pretty sure his wife's name was Daisy. He lived in Ben Lomond and taught at Santa Cruz High until he got in trouble for punching a kid. He told me the kid punched him first. They made him resign. I don't know where he went after that. We lost touch."

"He was teaching at San Lorenzo Valley High School for the last three years. Kate said he used to teach music, but the principal gave him an extra English class when the music program ended. What else do you know about Mac?"

"He was a lousy golfer, but boy could he play the drums."

As we sat together on the sofa, David's melodic voice drifted away like migrating butterflies until there was silence and the dream started. At first it was all sweet and simple—just Al wearing homemade wings made out of cardboard. He jumped off the roof of a garage, landed in the river and floated away. A menacing four-legged creature emerged from the far side of the river and chased after Albert, leaping and splashing until they both disappeared around a bend. Tab stood next to me pushing buttons on her electronic device, trying to control the creature chasing Al. When that didn't work, she collapsed on the ground sobbing.

I woke up on the couch feeling sad. David had gone home. The hall light was on, thanks to my sweet fiancé, so I trundled off to bed hoping to dream about my sweetheart instead of strange creatures.

Chapter 4

Looking forward to another visit with Aunt Clara, I charged through my house Monday morning collecting bottles of water and treats for Solow. We piled into the cab of my sweet little Mazda pickup and rolled onto Otis Drive. The sun rose behind us, and the Pacific Ocean beckoned from the West. Solow sat at my side, as last night's dreams of David danced in my head. When the cab became toasty warm, I put the windows down and my extra-long basset hung his head outside, ears and tongue flapping in the wind.

Fifty-five minutes later, we arrived in the bustling miniature metropolis of Ben Lomond. I found a place to park, helped Solow out of his seat, walked him across the street and entered the theater. I left him there for a few minutes while I darted over to the market next door to purchase a cup of coffee. While I was gone, he made friends with Kate, Gypsy and several junior actors.

"He's a wonderful dog, Josephine," Kate laughed as Gypsy crawled over Solow's long body, examining every inch of his handsomeness as he pretended to sleep.

Alicia walked in looking like an off-duty runway model wearing cut-offs, tank top and flip flops. She had pulled her pageboy haircut back into a mini ponytail and drizzled water from her water bottle across her shoulders.

Trigger ran past his mother and swooned over his pal, Solow. Kate had never met Alicia's son, but immediately put him to work making tree branches out of paper maché. Trigger looked happy to be helping.

Solow was finally able to take his morning nap in peace, under the worktable.

The old building had cooled off about ten degrees from yesterday's heat but seemed to be warming up all over again. I thought about poor Mac in the steaming hot attic as I sprinkled drinking water from a plastic bottle over my shoulders and a splash down the front of my shirt. The water drizzled down my body all the way to my sandals. Maybe Mac hadn't had water on hand and maybe he had been too hot to struggle.

Alicia and I climbed our ladders and finished drawing the last of the scenery before noon. I finally realized why the theater was so quiet. The carpenters were nowhere to be seen. I asked Kate why they weren't around.

"Because the children are practicing their songs and dances Monday, Tuesday, Wednesday and Thursdays. They don't need all that construction racket going on."

"What about last Friday?"

Kate looked up at the light fixtures attached to the ceiling for a moment. "Frank was here in the afternoon, and I think George was here all day."

"Don't mind me, Kate; just thinking about Mac's last day on earth. Do you know if Clara's coming in today?"

"She and Ben were going to take a ride down to Carmel. She's looking for a special fabric. She said to tell you she'll see you Friday. I think she wants you to stay with them…."

"Yeah, I'm planning to be there," I said, as Alicia handed me my purse. "Are you going to lunch, Kate?"

She shook her head, "I have errands to run. See you guys Friday." She scooped up Gypsy as she closed in on Solow's newest quiet place under one of the craft tables. The little scooter baby had followed my dog each time he found a new place to fall asleep.

Trigger, who had stripped down to soccer shorts and flip flops, took Solow by his leash and walked with his mother across the street to claim a picnic table in the park while I shopped for sandwiches at the market. As I waited for my order to be filled, grateful for cool grocery store air, I noticed Al stocking a deli shelf across the aisle with ready-made sandwiches. I walked over and congratulated him on his new job.

"Thanks," he said. "It's not hard work. I just have to remember to get stuff lined up with the right price stickers…."

"What's Tab doing today?"

"Ah…she doesn't feel too good." He kept his head down, concentrating on a tub of pre-made sandwiches. "She sorta stayed home." He looked everywhere but at me.

"Oops, my order's up. See ya later, Al."

I dropped three sandwiches into my basket on top of drinks and chips, paid for everything at the register and hoofed it across the street to a shaded table being serenaded by a lazy river. After a leisurely lunch, Alicia and Trigger walked back to the theater.

Instead of going back to work, I walked a few yards to the wire fence and enjoyed a moment of sunlight sparkling on water, earthy creek smells, deep shadows, and someone hopping the rocks way down river. I recognized that person and she didn't look sick to me. Maybe Tab had given up on finding a part in the play and Al was making an excuse for her.

As Tabatha disappeared around the bend in the river, a big, tall guy wearing a long-sleeved green shirt and rolled-up black pants suddenly appeared from the shadows, stepped into the water and disappeared around the bend.

Should I ignore what I saw, and pretend Tabatha wasn't being followed? That wasn't going to happen. All I knew was, if I didn't look for Tab and anything happened to her, I would never forgive myself.

Stretching my legs to the limit, Solow and I ran to my truck and leaped in.

He shivered, sensing my distress.

I peeled out, ran the one traffic light in town and parked in someone's driveway half a block from the bridge. We leaped to the ground and headed back to the familiar dirt path leading down to the river. Calling to Solow to follow me, I looked up as he slid down the hill, landing against my knees, knocking me flat. He licked my face.

"Good grief!" I groaned as I leaped up as fast as a voluptuous fifty-year-old woman can. "Come on, Solow, we have to catch Tab."

Solow followed me closely as we navigated the shoreline, waded for a while, and then ran on dry land dodging tree trunks and underbrush such as poison oak. When the water came up to my knees, Solow had to swim. We passed the bend in the river and came to a sandy beach. A two-foot high rock wall stretched halfway across the river, making a nice wading area for kids playing in the cold, clear water. A cluster of moms sat on the beach soaking up the sun.

The first person I saw was a mom carrying beach towels and a big bag full of plastic toys, trying to corral her four-year-old son and toddler daughter so that they could go home. Struggling hard, she could never get hold of both of them at the same time. I approached the boy and held onto his arm while I asked the poor woman if she had seen a teenage girl go by. She looked at me like I had just asked her about Einstein's Theory of Relativity, but thanked me for hanging onto her son.

"I saw her," a young voice behind me announced.

Turning around, I questioned a boy about Trigger's age. He patted Solow's head as he told me the girl had gone further down river and around the next bend.

"Was someone following her?"

"No."

"You're sure?"

"I'm sure."

Maybe the guy following her didn't want to be seen by anyone and stayed away from the beach area. I imagined there were plenty of deer trails throughout the forest. Solow and I stepped into the shallow water and sloshed along until we found another section of beach to walk on. As we took the next bend, I noticed a two-story house high above us, to our left. Redwoods surrounded the structure except for a perfect view of the river from a wrap-around wooden deck.

Movement caught my eye, someone on the deck wearing shorts and a tank top. Yep, that was Tab. We had come this far, might as well climb up the hill and talk to her.

Solow sniffed out a steep path leading to Tabatha, probably thinking of her as another potential admirer.

She saw us coming and waved.

Suddenly two German Shepherds appeared on the deck.

"Watch out for the poison oak!" Tabatha yelled.

"Yeah, avoid the poison oak and get chewed up by the dogs," I whispered to Solow, who had already run straight through a nasty patch of red-leafed trouble. I skirted the bush and climbed the last few yards of trail, ending at a wooden staircase leading up to the deck.

Tab thundered down the stairs, greeted us and walked us up to a cluster of outdoor furniture and two beautiful German Shepherds. She pointed one finger at the dogs. "Stay."

"How did you know where I live?" she asked, smiling.

Still watching the dogs, I said, "I didn't; we followed you…."

The sweetness in her voice suddenly evaporated. "Why would you do that?"

"Because a guy was following you and it wasn't your brother. I was concerned for your safety, that's all."

"That was very sweet of you, Josephine. Is this your dog?"

"Yep, this is Solow."

Sitting motionless against the house, the shepherds watched as Tabatha rubbed Solow's long velvety ears. "Look, I found a foxtail in his ear." She held up the little rocket-shaped grass seed that had the potential to cause serious trouble in a dog's ear.

"Thanks, Tab, nice work. Anyway, I wanted to tell you that this really tall guy was following you, but we lost him at the first beach."

"I don't know who that would be, like, we don't know many people around here…yet," she shivered in the hot sun.

Still keeping an eye on the dogs, I leaned against the redwood railing. Solow and I were taking in the sounds and smells of the river, while Tab sat on a lounge chair tanning her legs. We talked about silly subjects like her new nail polish, favorite movies and her young parents shipping off to Alaska to work in the oil industry. It seemed to me that Tabatha and Albert were collateral damage, destined to live with their mother's older sister, Daisy.

The two German Shepherds never moved.

Eventually the subject of Mac's murder came up.

"I have to go to Mac's funeral next week," Tabatha announced. "Aunt Daisy calls it a celebration of life. I call it a waste of time. She's already told my brother and me that we have to go, and we will because Aunt Daisy isn't so bad. Like, where's your dog?"

I looked around, suddenly realizing I hadn't seen Solow since shortly after we arrived about a half hour ago. I called him, expecting to hear his nails clippity clopping across the deck.

"He's not coming up to the deck so I'll have to go find him. See ya later, Tab."

One dog growled quietly, but the pair held their position.

A basset howled from at least a block away.

I clambered down the stairs, but before I hit the trail, I looked up and saw Tab leaning against the railing, wishing me luck.

I scurried down the path leading to the riverbank, and spotted Solow's paw prints in the damp sand. His intense howl told me he was on the trail of something or someone, but I worried because he knew nothing about Ben Lomond. I followed paw prints until the sand ended. Instead of wading into the water, I took a land route up a steep incline, probably a deer trail. Suddenly the brush opened up and there was a road.

I wiped sweat from my brow.

One car sped by, then two more.

Looking across the two lanes, I saw Solow's rear end disappear into a thicket. I darted across the street, climbed a dirt bank and tramped over someone's strawberry and rhubarb beds. A large country home at the end of a long driveway stood quietly in full shade, backed up to the mighty forest.

Leaving the house and civilization behind, I pushed my way through an opening in the underbrush, making it big enough for my mature figure to crawl through.

The trail zigzagged upward.

I called Solow.

He howled.

I tried to hurry but the ubiquitous redwoods, bays and pines sharing acreage with a billion waist-high ferns kept me at a humble pace. All Solow had to do was trot along under the greenery. After precious minutes of struggling up hill, things got worse. I had to weave my way around huge patches of blackberry bushes, prickly shrubs and poison oak.

Scratched and panting, I sat down on a fallen rotting redwood trying to catch my breath. A minute later, I spotted a three-foot high tunnel running through dense foliage a few yards up the mountain. Solow would have no problem moving through it, but for me it wasn't so easy. Crawling on hands and knees, my hair caught on low branches, my legs were scratched and scraped and on top of all that, I had a burr in my sandal.

I called Solow every minute or so. When the path finally opened up I sat down on a large rock, puffing air while emptying my sandal. A howl came from at least a hundred yards away. That was the moment I realized I couldn't hear the river anymore. In fact I hadn't heard it for quite awhile. The terrain had changed a bit, pines becoming the majority and redwoods the minority, no more ferns, just prickly shrubs and large boulders.

Later, sitting on a rock catching my breath, I checked my watch. It was six-thirty. Even if I headed for Ben Lomond at that moment, it would be dark when I got there. Besides, I couldn't go back without Solow. I would have to persevere.

When I finally reached sunlight at the top of the mountain, I turned around, shielded my eyes against the setting sun and looked out over the trail I had just climbed. All I saw was mountain range after mountain range. Turning my back to the fiery ball, I looked east at more mountain ranges. For one minute, I allowed myself to feel good about hiking to the top of a mountain, and then there was dread. What if a wild animal found Solow before I did?

I called him for the millionth time.

Solow's howl sounded far away, down the eastern slope, on the dark side of the mountain.

My eyes adjusted to twilight-mode and with gravity in my favor, I began to descend the eastern side of the mountain one tired shaky step at a time. Carefully I dodged boulders and prickly bushes but managed to stumble and roll into a huckleberry bush.

An owl hooted—another hooted back. I guessed they were talking about me and rolling their eyes.

I picked myself up and tried the steep decline again. But that is all I remember.

Chapter 5

Morning arrived. The sun was up, songbirds were singing and I was wrapped around a boulder the size of a breadbox. According to my level of body stiffness, I had slept all night in that position, possibly from losing consciousness from a fall I couldn't remember. I felt the top of my head where it hurt. Ouch! Blinking and squinting at the rising sun, I gazed across a deep valley to another range of mountains covered in redwood trees.

Thinking about how beautiful nature was, I sucked in some cool air, sat up and stretched. Ouch! Slowly I stood. More ouches. My whole body was unhappy, not to mention filthy from rolling in the dirt. At least my mind worked. It occurred to me that it was now Tuesday, my day off. I did a re-wind and thought about Monday, painting at the theater, chasing after Tab and then chasing Solow. Focusing on what was most important, I looked around for Solow. I opened my mouth to call him. "Ouch." Even my jaw hurt.

A hawk circled above. I purposely moved my fingers to let him know I wasn't dead. He moved on. The air was clean and still. A jumbo jet moved silently upward across the pure blue sky, creating a long white trail as it moved in a southerly direction. I figured it had taken off from San Francisco and would probably land in LA. I watched the modern marvel until it disappeared, until there were no signs whatsoever of modern man—or even humans, period.

As I climbed about a hundred yards up the rocky dirty mountain, my body warmed and became stronger and more limber. But I was a long way from being a mountain climber, a fact that was reinforced every time my foot slipped off a rock or my hands failed to find something to grip. With one step back for every two steps forward, I finally reached the wonderful semi-flatness of the top of the mountain. After a quick look around and a few unanswered calls to Solow, I began my trek down the western slope.

My heart ached. Where was Solow? I hadn't heard a howl or bark since the night before.

Down hill was pretty easy, just go with gravity and don't get snagged by low-hanging branches. Unlike the eastern side of the mountain, the western side was awash in redwoods, foliage and dead leaves up to my ankles. At times the terrain leveled, but not for long. Mostly it was a down hill slip and slide trip.

Since I didn't see any signs of roads or paths on the way up, I was surprised to come across a dirt road carved into the mountainside. It might have been a logging road that had obviously not been used in at least a hundred years. I hoped the road would take me to the bottom of the mountain.

A dirt road was better than nothing, but this one had obstacles at every turn, where parts of it had been washed out and where slides made it almost impassable. Wanting to go west, the road I found ran north to south. Not having a coin to toss, I chose to head north but wondered if I should have gone south. Finally I came to a switchback where the road made a tight left downward turn. Shortly after that, it made a quick right downward turn. The switchbacks continued until, when I stopped and listened, I was able to hear a dull roar coming from Highway Nine traffic a few miles away, down in the valley.

Yesterday was on my mind, images of leaping out of the truck, leaving the doors unlocked and my purse inside the cab. But the thought that hurt most was what happened to Solow. People always talked about cougars roaming the mountains, but I refused to think about them, mostly.

As I daydreamed about finding my sweet basset, the road came to a fork. Should I go right or left? To the right was a continuation of the switchbacks, but the road to the left was different—a kinder, gentler road. It was flat, straight and lined on both sides with dozens of very tall palm trees, an anomaly for sure. Sunlight filtered through the palms, sprinkling light across acres of fluorescent green ferns bordered by deep green forest. Naturally this was the road for me.

All the road needed was to be paved in yellow bricks instead of layers of dead leaves.

I laughed out loud.

A minute later, I heard the crunch of leaves, stopped and looked around for wild animals. Farther down the road, I thought I saw something move in the distance. It looked like a man walking his dog. Was it a mirage? Still in the "Land of Oz," my logical mind was slow to focus.

The mystical dog barked and began running toward me, ears flying like whirligigs. I couldn't believe my eyes. The dog had Solow's short bowed legs and long rabbit ears.

It was Solow. What a happy reunion! I felt like I would float up to the treetops with happiness as I squatted on the ground hugging my sweet basset. But who was the guy walking him? And why did the man wear long sleeves and long pants on a hot summer day? The closer he came, the taller he looked. He looked like he was in his early twenties, athletic but strange somehow. His bare feet were twice the size of mine, but the look on his face didn't scare me. And I trusted Solow's choices of friends.

"Hello, my name is Josephine and this is Solow." I gave my baby another hug and stood up. Craning my neck, I realized that this man was at least two heads taller than my five-foot-six frame and was as tall as the tallest big league basketball players. His mysterious pale blue eyes looked at my feet. Was he shy or afraid of me?

"Josephine, your strap is broken," his deep baritone voice cut through the quiet forest like a chainsaw.

"Huh? Oh, my sandal, yeah, I guess it is." It was no wonder after all the hiking and climbing I had done. "Where am I?"

"We're standing about three miles up from the San Lorenzo River. Do you need help…."

"Oh no, just point the way and we'll go back to Ben Lomond. Wait a minute, I just thought of something…what are you doing up here…with my dog?"

He laughed nervously. "My name is Paul and I live up here, but I'd appreciate it if you didn't tell anyone."

"Okay, Paul, does anyone else know you're up here?"

"Just Daisy."

"You mean Tabatha's aunt?"

He nodded.

I looked around and finally spotted a pointy rooftop peeking over the tops of palm trees about a hundred yards away, not the lean-to I was expecting. Paul saw that I had discovered his abode and explained that it was a turn-of-the-century abandoned hotel. It had served as a refuge for oil barons and swells of all sorts, a playground for the very rich until the crash in 1929. Paul explained that business had dried up and the hotel was boarded up in 1932. Obviously, the world had forgotten its existence.

Feeling a bit faint from the lack of yesterday's lunch and dinner and today's breakfast, I was torn between getting back to town and possibly seeing the grand hotel for myself.

"Your dog likes oatmeal." Paul shuffled his feet, reached one long arm in my direction and pulled a leaf out of my hair.

"Oh really, I didn't know that. I know he loves bacon…."

"Doesn't everybody?" he chuckled. "I guess you want to see the hotel, right?"

"Well, if you insist. And maybe a glass of water."

"No problem," he said, as he strolled along the wide leaf-covered path.

I had to walk briskly just to keep up with Paul.

Solow bounced along, his tail wagging.

We finally arrived at an overgrown used-to-be hedge with an ornate wrought-iron gate in the middle that opened into an extensive entry garden full of weeds and way overgrown bushes, but still beautiful in a wild sort of way. We passed an empty fish pond and a large rusty aviary leaning to one side. Unruly rose bushes grew in a row along the front of a very long porch, big enough to hold a dozen junior soccer teams and all their parents.

"What's the matter, Josephine?"

"Nothing, your home is amazing…a three-story Victorian." I knew my jaw was dragging, but I couldn't help it. Of course all the paint was gone and the porch sagged at one end. The first- and second-story windows had boards nailed across them, but the third-story windows still boasted original etched glass, some with stained-glass designs.

"Actually, it's four stories. The kitchen is in the underground basement," Paul said as he led the way up wide stone steps, across an uneven wooden porch and opened a squeaky front door for me.

It was easy to imagine beautifully dressed people lounging on the porch, playing cards, discussing the weather. I admired the contours of a once beautiful set of doors. As I entered the foyer, I noticed the scent of old wood, pipe tobacco, and something sweet from long, long ago. Suddenly I was five years old in my grandmother's house where the wood floors squeaked and a friendly fire burned in the fireplace. It was a peaceful place, socked away in my heart.

Paul left the room, came back with a paper cup of water and handed it to me. I looked around for something to sit on.

"Josephine, you look exhausted. Let's sit down in the next room." He motioned for me to follow him.

The next room was much larger than the first. The main feature of the six-sided room was a long built-in counter, giving in to old age as it sloped down to the floor at one end. Cobwebs were everywhere. Most of the fine furniture had fallen to pieces, but one built-in bench carved out of a solid piece of redwood and back-lit by three partially covered windows, looked sturdy enough for a quick sit.

Solow sniffed every corner of the room while Paul answered my questions, beginning with, why do you live here and how do you know Daisy?

"Mac and Daisy raised me." He looked at the floor. "I was about five when I wandered over to their house," he laughed. "Because I was 'different,' Daisy didn't want to turn me over to the authorities. Mac didn't want anything to do with me, but he relented and I stayed. I couldn't speak and I was already as big as a ten-year-old. Daisy home-taught me for the next twelve years, right up until Tabatha and Albert arrived."

I choked on the water, delicious as it was. "So that makes you seventeen? And on your own because of them?"

"Yep, and I'm still different, can't get a job…so I live up here."

"How do you eat?"

"Daisy leaves food out for me," he shrugged.

"Why did you have to leave?"

"Because I was a secret the rest of the family didn't know about. Mac and Daisy never invited family over or anyone for that matter. Mac was too embarrassed, and Daisy wanted to protect me from people's cruel remarks. She taught me how to grow food, cook, do basic carpentry and lots of math, science and history. But it was time for me to leave."

"I thought Mac was the teacher…."

"Yeah, but he didn't want to teach me."

"Where did you come from?"

"Like I said, I was only five, but I remember living in the mountains with my parents in a dank, dark place. That winter there was a rainstorm that lasted for days and days and then a big mudslide happened. Next thing I know I'm alone, so I wandered down the mountain, all the way to Daisy's door."

"I haven't met her yet but she sounds like a very nice lady."

"Yeah…so right away she runs a bath for me, but I hid behind the sofa. I had never seen the inside of a house or a bathtub before. I remember feeling very scared but not of Daisy, just Mac and all the strange things in the house."

"Did Mac ever hurt you?"

"No, he ignored me." Paul took my empty cup and set it on the long counter where people a hundred years ago had signed the registry for their stay at the hotel. He sat down on the bench beside me.

"Did you get along with the German Shepherds?" I asked.

"Daisy gave them to me on my tenth birthday. They were my playmates. I trained them."

"So why were you following Tabatha down the river?"

"Daisy doesn't get out much, and I can't help feeling responsible for Tabatha's safety. She's young, new in town and doesn't know anything about Ben Lomond…."

"Are you saying she's not safe in…."

"I'm just saying, I'm going to keep an eye on her because Daisy can't. She has seizures and arthritis and some other stuff. I trained the dogs to help her."

"Is that right?" I said, halfway believing him.

After a few minutes of sitting on the bench, I felt fairly rested.

Paul gave me a tour of the place. The basic bones of the building seemed to be strong since it was mostly built using large redwood beams. The floors were redwood and hardly squeaked at all, but the once lovely rugs had deteriorated into strings and rags.

The more delicate furniture had turned into kindling. I recognized some of it stacked by the fireplace in Paul's bedroom on the top floor where he had a great view of the grounds and plenty of sunshine pouring through very old blown-glass windows framed in hand-carved walnut.

A sleeping bag was spread across the floor and several stacks of books stood beside tattered wallpaper. I leaned my head sideways to read the titles. Most were textbooks on botany, biology, electronics, history and philosophy. For fun, there were classics like *Gone With the Wind, War and Peace* and *Anna Karenina*.

"Daisy let me have as many books as I wanted. Took me a lot of trips at night to get them up here."

"Wasn't it hard to find your way at night?"

"She gave me a flashlight, but I didn't need it. I see pretty well at night."

Everywhere I looked the hotel spoke of luxury and the good old days. Even the water I drank had tasted exceptionally good. Paul told me he collected it from a spring on the property.

As we descended a couple of staircases to the main floor, I asked Paul how he found the place and why was he able to live there.

"Josephine, I don't exactly have permission. I'm just taking it a day at a time. I don't know how long I'll be able to live here, but I'm not vandalizing the place, I'm actually fixing things. I found a hammer and nails in the basement and an old rusty saw in the garden shed."

"Have Tabatha or Albert ever seen you?"

"Yes, only once, but it was dark and I was high up in a tree by the theater. I think they spotted me but not enough to get a good look."

"That was the night Mac went missing, right?"

"Right."

"Did you see who locked him in the attic?"

Paul cringed. "Nope."

"Okay, well I'm going to go now. How do I get back to Ben Lomond?"

"Just take the switchback lumber road you were on. It's better than sliding down the mountain on your backside."

"Thanks. Nice meeting you, Paul."

"Same here." He gave Solow a good pat and waved goodbye from the front porch as we set off for town with one sandal flapping.

Chapter 6

Solow and I pounded down the logging trail until it narrowed and ended above a very high cliff. I looked around and finally found what looked like a deer trail leading downward into a neighborhood of cabins converted into year-round homes. The little houses had large properties, no fences and plenty of shade from the pervasive redwoods.

Cutting across someone's back yard, we came upon a woman taking out the garbage.

"Oh, you startled me," she said, dropping the bag of garbage a bit short of a tall blue garbage can. We looked down at the rotting stinking produce lying on the ground.

"Sorry," I said. "That garbage would make good compost."

She forced a grin. "I'm too busy for that nonsense. We have plenty of compost everywhere under these trees." She swung her pointy finger around the area.

"Yeah, I guess you're right. Can you tell me how to get to the road into Ben Lomond?"

The woman pointed to a set of brick stairs at the far end of her property. Taking the little stairs two at a time, I imagined Paul taking them three or four at a time. I wondered how he got to town without being seen—a question for another day.

The steps ended at the edge of a familiar-looking road just outside of Ben Lomond. One block and we were standing in front of my truck. I peeked in the window and there was my purse. The doors were still unlocked so I helped Solow into his seat, climbed into mine and drove three blocks over to the theater and parked.

Since it was Tuesday afternoon, the entrance doors were open and the building rocked with music. I left Solow in the cab with the windows down, and walked past the open theater doors where seventy-something kids sat in a circle three-deep on the floor, singing a song I never heard before. After one quick look, I marched over to the grocery store for a meal, heading straight for the deli aisle. I put in an order for two Mountain Man sandwiches, hold the onions.

"Hey, Josephine, what are you doing here on a Tuesday?" Albert asked.

I turned around. "Hi, Al. I see you're working hard. Solow and I are just grabbing a bite to eat and looking around the town. How's Tab?"

"Girls! I guess she's fine." He rolled his eyes and went back to stuffing the shelf with bags of cookies.

My name was called, I picked up my order and stood in line at the checkout. A young woman named Maggi waited on me, took my money and asked if I knew my forehead was bleeding.

"Huh?" I touched my head and looked at my hand. Nothing.

"Looks like dried blood," she said as she handed me my change. "Were you in that, 'Save the Steelhead' off-road bike race this morning?"

"Ah, yeah, guess that's why I'm so hungry. Thanks!"

Tired and hungry, I walked toward the truck concentrating very hard not to spill or drop any parts of our lunch.

Solow howled.

I looked up, and there was Kate walking toward me with Gypsy strapped to her back. "Kate, working on a Tuesday?" I said.

"Janinne and I are meeting someone here at two o'clock for an audition...what happened to you, Josephine? Fall off your bike?" She plucked a small branch from my hair.

"Yeah, as a matter of fact I hit the dirt pretty hard," I chuckled.

"I got a strange call last night... Alicia asking if I had seen you...what's that about?"

"Ah, no problem," I said as my stomach growled. "She's like a mother hen and I forgot to tell her where I was going."

"Well, take care, Josephine. Here comes my gal."

I followed her glance, and there was Tab crossing the street.

"You found a part for her?"

"Yes, if she can do it. It requires a couple of solos..." Kate turned her head. "Hi, Tab," she said. "Follow me."

I climbed into my truck, unwrapped one sandwich for Solow and ripped open the other one for me. When had anything ever tasted that good? Solow had inhaled his whole lunch by the time I ate the first half of my sandwich and washed it down with iced tea. I poured water into an empty paint container for my buddy. The minute our little picnic ended, I remembered my phone. Pulling it out of my purse, I immediately saw that it was dead and plugged it into the dash. Had Alicia or David called me to find out why I mysteriously disappeared?

As I thought about Alicia, my truck automatically made all the right turns heading south until we were parked in her neighborhood across the street from her house. By that time, my phone had two bars so I dropped it into my purse.

We climbed out of the truck. Solow pulled on his leash, anxious to see the family and their little sheltie named Tansey.

Sure enough, Tansey heard us coming and barked her head off until Alicia opened the front door and let us in. My best friend looked like she was somewhere between fainting with relief and using my head for batting practice.

"Where have you been?" she gasped. "I've been calling everyone…."

"I'm sorry, Allie. It happened so fast and I just had to go. I'm sorry I worried you."

"Sit down, Jo; you look awful." She pointed to the sofa in the living room.

I sat down and sniffed the air. Mmm—enchiladas.

"Have you looked in a mirror lately…?"

"Allie, you're beginning to sound like my mother. I guess you want to know what happened to us yesterday."

"Yeah, that would be nice," she growled. "I called your folks last night…."

"Oh boy; were they upset?"

"No, I just said I was looking for you, nothing serious."

"Thanks, Allie. Anyway, yesterday I thought I saw someone following Tabatha down the river."

"Like the last time?" She rolled her eyes.

"Kinda like that, but this time there wasn't anyone, but I did see where Tabatha lives and talked to her a bit. Then I realized that Solow wasn't around. I went looking for him."

"For two days?"

"Kinda. I heard him barking and followed the sound up the mountain. You wouldn't believe how big those mountains are. I kept hearing him but couldn't catch up. A lot of it was really steep and dense with underbrush.

It took hours to get to the top and when I finally got there, I stopped and listened. It sounded like Solow's bark came from the eastern side of the mountain, the rocky steep side. I remember being so tired that I thought going down hill would be a break. But I only took a few steps and my sandal slipped. I rolled the rest of the way, smack into a boulder and slept all night curled up with a rock."

Alicia's cocky smile morphed into a look of concern. "Were you hurt?" She stared at my forehead. "Are you all right, Jo?"

"I'm fine. I was a little disoriented when I woke up this morning, but later I found Solow and we made it back to Ben Lomond. Can you believe it, my truck was unlocked the whole time and my purse was on the seat. I love that little town."

Alicia believed my story—the half that I confessed. Part of me hoped she wouldn't believe what I told her because even to me the story made me sound unstable or at the very least, temporarily unhinged. Because I had made a promise to Paul, the rest of the story was not revealed. But that was the best part—the interesting young man and the beautiful but elderly hotel nestled away among dozens of palm trees. The builder must have brought the trees up from Los Angeles. It was lucky for Paul that the encroaching redwood forest ensured secrecy from land and air.

"Jo, are you worried about something?"

"No, he'll be fine…."

"Who will be fine?" Alicia cocked her head and gave me "the mom stare."

"Oh, ah, Solow of course. He was fine when I found him. We both need a bath, but otherwise we're okay." I ran a hand over the top of my head and pulled a couple of burrs from my tangled hair.

"Did you go to the theater today?" she asked.

"Not really…just passed by it. Kate was there. She and Janinne were about to have Tab audition for a role in the play. I sure hope she gets the part. She's a sweet kid."

"Yeah, but you need to stop following her…."

"I know, my imagination gets me into trouble sometimes," I admitted. It felt good to be in Alicia's kid-friendly, animal-friendly, smells-like-enchiladas home. My eyelids felt so heavy. I rested my head on the back of the couch. Alicia said something but I couldn't make sense of it.

***

When I woke up to Beethoven's Fifth blaring from my phone, it was already dark outside. I must have slept about five hours. Alicia and family had already finished their dinner, but she had saved a couple of chicken enchiladas for me. The phone call was from David wondering where I was. Too sleepy to explain everything, I just told him I was visiting with the Quintanas and promised to spend time with him the next day.

Driving home after a good nap, I decided to stop at the Eastside Watsonville grocery store and pick up a sack of kibble for Solow. I found my favorite employee stocking the dairy aisle.

"Josephine…what happened to you? Fall off a bike or something?"

"Nice to see you too, Robert. And yes, I did fall off a bike…once upon a time," I mumbled. I was beginning to believe it really happened.

Robert, plump and freckled, but full of youthful energy and a good work ethic, turned back to loading the shelves with half-gallon cartons of milk.

"How are your niece and nephew?" I asked, remembering Molly's antics and Mick's endless energy, and feeling glad there weren't any hyperactive ten-year-old twins in my family.

"They're out of my hair at last. Sometimes I actually miss them. My sister moved to Felton, and the kids are in a theater group four whole days a week."

"Is the theater in Ben Lomond?"

"Yeah, I think it is. They seem to like it up there. Did you hear about a guy getting murdered…?"

"Yep, as a matter of fact, I'm painting props at the theater in Ben Lomond because it was their Mac who was murdered. They say he was a great painter."

"So who did it?"

"Not sure, but I have a couple of people in mind." I tossed a carton of cottage cheese into my basket. "What's good in produce today?"

"Avocados and spinach," he said, grabbing a half gallon of orange juice in each hand. "The raspberries are good too."

"Thanks, Robert."

"No problem. You stay safe up there in Ben Lomond."

"Don't worry, it's a very safe little town—except for one little murder."

Chapter 7

I crawled out of bed and peeked through the curtains. Either I was going blind or dense cotton candy fog had filled up the whole outside world. It wasn't unusual to have fog in the summer. Every year it kept us guessing, as the weather lurched from warm sunny days to fog-filled mornings that sometimes stayed that way for the whole day—for days at a time.

My cell phone showed the time to be nine o'clock. I couldn't remember ever sleeping that late. I had taken a leisurely bath the night before, sending tons of dirt and debris down the drain. I remembered feeling so light and clean as I slipped on my pajamas and dried my hair. I had promised David I would call him back, but instead I crawled under the covers and slept for ten hours.

Someone pounded on my back door. I quickly pinched my cheeks, ran fingers through my hair and made a quick stop at the bathroom where I gulped and spit some blue gargle liquid into the sink. From there it was a few quick steps into the kitchen and into David's arms.

"You're just getting up? Sorry, honey; I can come back later…."

"Yes, come back later, but stay for a minute. I need my big bear hug. I missed you."

"I missed you too. I was beginning to wonder if you still lived here," he chuckled. "I let Solow out an hour ago, but you just kept sleeping. Did you know that you talk in your sleep?"

"No, what did I say?"

"It was pretty crazy. Apparently you were having this dream about a mansion with palm trees. I couldn't understand what you were saying half the time."

Good, I thought.

"I slept so soundly, I don't remember anything," I yawned.

"Your mom called and invited us to dinner tonight, since you're busy on the weekends now."

"What did you tell her?"

"That I hadn't seen you but would pass the message along. I wonder why she didn't call you in the first place."

"She tried to, but my phone was dead...Alicia told me."

"Josie, I was wondering if you'd like to go bowling with me today. There's this little bowling place in downtown Gilroy, not too crowded and they have great food. If you want we could have a late breakfast there and then bowl a couple of games."

"That sounds like fun. Give me twenty minutes." I walked David three steps to the back door and we kissed. As soon as the door closed behind him, I ran to my room to figure out something to wear. What does one wear to a bowling match? I hadn't bowled in eighteen years, not since my husband Marty was alive. I picked out a pair of navy blue knee-length pants, a yellow sleeveless blouse and navy sandals. On my way out I grabbed my "go-everywhere" white cardigan in case the fog persisted, stuffed a pair of shorty white socks into my pants pocket and wondered if the rented shoes would be as ugly as they were eighteen years ago.

David was right about the food and I was right about the shoes. Our bowling was atrocious because everything was funny after just one mimosa with brunch. Historically, one glass of anything gave me the giggles. Fortunately, we had the place to ourselves, except for three vintage women having their own cackle-fest at the far end of the ten-lane facility.

Sandwiched in between the morning leagues that ended at noon and the next league starting at two in the afternoon, we had plenty of time and room. During the middle of our second game, the three old ladies from "down yonder" shuffled over to a table behind us and ordered tea. After a few minutes of observation, one of the ladies left her tea and took the two steps down to our benches. As I watched David smash his ball into seven of the ten pins, the old woman sat down next to me.

"It's all in the wrist, dear," she said, holding up one ancient wrinkly hand, twisting it back and forth in the air. "You need a bit of a curve."

"Thanks for the tip," I said with a snort that burst into a giggle. "Sorry, I had a mimosa with my brunch…."

"I understand, dear; my Freddy's a lush."

That did it—I could no longer control my giggle maker. Even the old lady was howling. We both stood up and whooped and hollered when David obliterated the last three pins standing. He turned and informed me it was my turn.

I pulled myself together, raised my ten-pound borrowed baby-blue ball, took three steps and let her go.

"Crash!"

Everyone gawked at the explosion of ten pins going in all directions. Cheers and whistles came from the tea-drinkers. My advisor congratulated me with a slap on the back and walked out of the building with her friends.

But she was back a few minutes later. She sat down in the seat next to me.

"I guess our white sweaters look a lot alike," she laughed as she hung my sweater across the back of the seat. "When I got outside, I realized I didn't even bring mine—why would you need a sweater in the middle of summer?"

"Because I live in Aromas, and it was fogged in this morning."

"Oh my goodness, sorry I butted into your business, dear. Everyone calls me "Busybody Bessie.' No surprise," she laughed.

"I'm Josephine Stuart and this is…."

"The Josephine Stuart who paints murals?"

"Ah, yeah, that's me."

"You painted a lovely undersea mural for my grandson and his bride about ten years ago. They live in Morgan Hill…." Bessie waited a moment for me to remember that particular mural out of the hundreds I had painted over the years. When I finally nodded, she asked where I was currently painting.

"Actually, I'm painting theater props in Ben Lomond…."

"You don't say! I lived in Felton for many years, and I know all about the Park Theater in Ben Lomond and the wonderful plays. Janinne was my neighbor and we're still friends. She told me the terrible news about poor Mac…not that he didn't deserve…oh never mind. Bet it was his girlfriend that did him in," she grumbled.

"Who was his girlfriend?" I asked, trying not to show my intense interest.

"Some younger blond teacher at the high school. I don't remember her name." Bessie looked up toward the shoe rental counter. "Oops, gotta go, dear. Lovely meeting you," she said as she stood and marched up the two steps to join her friends who had come back to get her.

I ran after her. "Bessie, wait!"

She turned around to face me.

"What subjects does the blond teach?"

Bessie laughed, "Biology, naturally."

"Thanks…take care."

Driving home, David asked how work was going.

"Good, but it's a challenge drawing such a variety of settings and characters. I can't wait to see it all come together. Right now I can't imagine how it will, but everyone I talk to raves about Janinne's writing. And the whole crew really knows what they're doing. You'll never guess the name of the play."

"Okay, I give up, tell me what it is," he chuckled.

"Peter Pamilton. Pretty crazy, don't you think?"

"So is it about Peter and the Wolf or Peter Pan or what?"

I thought about it for a moment as he turned the car up my driveway. "I think it's Peter Pan, at least part of the play—not sure about the rest. Janinne likes to really mix it up with other story lines." *Kind of like real life*, I thought, where so many things were happening all at once. Paul was living alone in the forest, Tab was trying out for a part in the play and I wondered if Daisy was missing Mac.

David opened the door for me, and we kissed goodbye.

"You're not coming in?" I whined.

"Nope, I promised I would help Emmet spread compost on his flower beds. Once I'm there, he'll find all kinds of things for me to do." Our neighbor, Emmet, was ninety years old and often needed help with heavy lifting chores. David was retired, strong, healthy and always willing.

"That's good because I need to give Solow a bath and I have laundry to catch up on." I walked toward the front door and Solow's insistent howling from inside.

"I'll pick you up at five-thirty. Would your mom like some salsa?"

"She would love some of your homemade apricot salsa. See you in three hours." David's orchard of apricots had ripened practically over night. He picked cots for hours everyday all week, and gave bags of the fruit to all our neighbors. He still had enough fruit to make salsa for the whole city of Santa Cruz. A manly man who could cultivate the land and cook up a gourmet meal—what more could I ask for? I tried to imagine us living together, married, me burning the food and David cleaning up my messes. I tended to drag my feet on choosing a wedding day even though I knew I was getting the best of the deal.

Solow followed me through the house as if I'd been gone for a week instead of a couple of hours of bowling.

I shoved a basket of whites into the washing machine, folded clean towels and sheets and tried to solve Mac's murder in my head. I had very few facts and no solid suspects so I grabbed a note pad and wrote down some unanswered questions.

1. How did Paul know about the abandoned hotel?
2. What kind of lock was used on the attic door?
3. What is Daisy like—did she murder Mac?
4. Was it a coincidence that Mac was killed just one week after Tabatha and Albert moved into his house?
5. Is there a way into the attic other than the stairs?
6. Does the building have a basement?

Obviously, the person Tab saw hiding in a tree next to the theater was Paul. What was he doing that night? I quickly scratched that question from my mind because I had great respect for the strange young man. Besides, he told me he was keeping Tab and Albert safe—but safe from what?

Solow opened his eyes and gave a friendly bark.

A moment later there was a tap, tap, on the front door.

"Oh my gosh, it's five-thirty already."

I opened the door for David, then darted down the hall to fetch my sweater and run a brush through my hair. As I returned to the kitchen, I heard kibble hitting Solow's bowl.

"Thanks, David. I guess we're ready to go."

After a comfortable forty-minute ride in David's sporty Miata, we entered Santa Cruz city limits and parked on Walnut Avenue in front of the well-kept bungalow I had grown up in. It practically rubbed elbows with Myrtle's house next door. Myrtle was a year or two older than my folks, who would enter their eighth decade of life in one more year. But "old" they were not. Dad had his bowling, Mom had her clubs and everything else they did together—such as roller blading, camping, hiking and sailing.

Mom greeted us at the door wearing her signature red sari and gold sandals.

"What's the occasion, Mom?"

"Myrtle's birthday, I thought you knew."

"Ah, yeah, and David brought her some apricot salsa."

Mom looked disappointed.

David stepped into the house. "I'm sure Myrtle will share it with you, Leola," he laughed.

Mom smiled and closed the door behind us. She had always liked David and couldn't understand why we weren't already married.

Dad stepped up and shook David's hand heartily. In my mind, the two men shared many admirable characteristics, excellent character being the main one.

"Bob, how's the bowling team doing?" David asked.

"Ya win some, ya lose some…."

David nodded knowingly.

As usual, the men settled on the sofa in front of the TV. The San Francisco Giants were playing.

Mom and I trotted into the kitchen where Myrtle sat at the breakfast bar sampling the wine. When our old friend saw me, she set her glass down and careened off the stool without incident, except that her curly black wig suddenly changed direction. She pushed a stray curl out of her eyes and gave me a welcoming hug. Her warm plumpness was wrapped tightly in a pale pink polyester pantsuit smelling of Tide and fabric softener.

"The roses are in your cheeks, my dear," Myrtle winked. She and Mom had been waiting impatiently for a ring and a wedding date. So far, I had the ring but had not set a date. Every time David brought up the subject, I ran the conversation off the tracks.

"Happy birthday, Myrtle, how have you been?"

"Older than dirt…other than that, I'm still kicking," she giggled, and took another gulp of wine. "Looks like you landed a job right in the middle of trouble."

"What do you mean, Myrtle—the murder?" I knew that she read the newspaper and kept up on everything that went on between the North end and the South end of Santa Cruz County.

"Murder is just part of it, dear…" Myrtle whispered when Mom left the room. "You might want to look into the San Lorenzo Valley Water Board."

Dinner with Myrtle definitely gave me something to chew on. I even chewed on it in my dreams that night as four men wearing black and white striped overalls argued about whether the reservoir water should be flavored to taste like soy sauce or peach pie. One man shouted that he would donate enough peaches for the project. Another man held up a tiny bottle of soy sauce, saying that his bottle was enough to flavor the whole lake.

Chapter 8

Solow watched me from across the room Thursday morning as I sprang out of bed and padded down the hall to the bathroom for a quick shower. My body was soapy wet, and my head was swimming with things to do, places to go and people to see. Myrtle had opened my eyes to murder suspects and their motives. After a quick oatmeal breakfast for me and kibble for Solow, we took off in the truck for Ben Lomond, not that I relished another long drive across the county. But I had to follow through on Myrtle's clues. Besides, it would be fun for Solow.

We arrived in Ben Lomond a couple of minutes after nine. I curbed the truck two blocks away from Park Theater as a long line of moms idled their SUVs, offloading little actors and actresses as close to the theater as they could get. Solow and I walked the two blocks and stood outside on the sidewalk while kids ran in every direction, mostly through the entrance doors. Kate and Gypsy were the last to arrive.

"Josephine, are you going in to watch?"

"No, I just needed to ask you about a couple of things."

"Shoot." I detected impatience in her voice.

Gypsy yawned and stretched her arms. "Bah…loooo."

"Did Tab get the part?"

"Did she ever! She has the voice of an angel," Kate smiled.

"How many people are on the San Lorenzo Valley Water Board and what are their names?"

Gypsy cooed as if she knew the answer.

"You got me on that one," Kate said. "I don't keep up with that stuff as well as I should—way too political for me."

"You can't think of any names?"

Kate moved closer to the open door as seventy-something cherubic voices sang a good morning song.

"I know there are five on the board, actually four now that Mac's gone. One is a woman, Shirley something…Logan, I think."

"Shirley Logan. Thank you, Kate; that's a start," I said, as she turned and entered the building. So she did know of at least one board member. I wondered if she knew the other three.

My next stop was down river at Daisy's house. Rather than hop rocks and sand bars to her back door, I decided to drive to her house and knock on the front door. As Solow and I cruised through the targeted neighborhood at three miles an hour, I checked each roadside mailbox. When I saw "Mackie" printed on the side of a standard silver mailbox, I knew we had found Mac's house.

Solow loved the ride but was happy to investigate and christen the mailbox post. He nosed around the flat front yard covered in mulchy leaves, native trees, one giant rhododendron pressed against the front of the house and a dirt path leading to the front door. The front of the wood frame house was one story at street level, but the back of the house, clinging to the hillside above the river, was two stories if you included a basement tucked below the deck.

We approached the front door. I knocked.

Deep-throated barking erupted. Obviously, the German Shepherds knew we had arrived. I heard a female voice say, “Quiet,” and suddenly they were. She opened the door and looked up at me. The German Shepherds crowded closer. She waved an arm and they backed away. One more wave and they were curled up in their beds next to the TV.

“I’m sorry…” Daisy said.

“My name is Josephine and this is Solow….”

“Oh, for heaven’s sake. Tabatha told me all about you.” She smiled. “Tab isn’t here right now….”

“That’s okay, I came to talk to you.”

Her little round face grew pinker. “Tab said you might ask questions about my husband’s murder. Unfortunately, I probably won’t be much help. Come in and sit.” She waved her hand toward the sofa.

Not to be out-done by two big dogs, I obediently sat down. Solow stood, pressed tightly to my calves, avoiding the four brown eyes staring at him from across the room.

“Were your dogs professionally trained?”

Daisy glanced at the ceiling. “No, not really….”

“Did your husband train them?”

“Ah, not really….”

“Was it Paul?”

Poor Daisy looked like she had suddenly discovered eight fingers on each of her chubby little hands. She finally looked up. Her eyes met mine as she squirmed in her armchair.

“Yes, it was Paul. Nobody knows about Paul. How do you know about him?” Her voice was softer than the tick of the grandfather clock in the corner.

“It’s a long story. I just want to commend you for the fine job you did raising him. He’s a smart cookie and sweet as pie.”

Daisy gulped and looked at the shaggy green carpet for a moment. “Paul had to leave and he was ready, but I wish he could have stayed,” she sniffed.

"The way I heard the story, it was Mac who didn't want anyone to know that Paul lived here. I admit the boy is different, with all that thick hair, over seven feet tall and the shape of his face, but if you're proud of the boy, maybe its time he met his aunts, uncles and cousins. Are there any relatives for him to meet?"

"Yes, a few relatives. I always wished we could be one big happy family. Keeping Paul a secret has meant the end of relations with my sister, my Aunt Silvia, Uncle Henry and so many others," she sighed. "Mac resented Paul for living with us, and I resented Mac for keeping me from my family—but I could never have turned little Pauly away."

"So your sister sent her kids over here to live with you?"

Daisy cocked her head, probably wondering where my information came from. "Yes, she pays for them to stay here, but I would take them no matter what. They're good kids. The part that hurts is not having Paul around."

"If it's any comfort, I had a real nice visit with Paul and he's doing fine."

"Thank you, Josephine; that means a lot. Would you care for a cup of tea?"

"That would be wonderful. Looks like the dogs are fine with each other." The three dogs had just finished a butt-sniffing session and gone back to their doggie beds for a nap. It looked like Solow had been officially accepted into their club.

"Paul has a way with animals," she smiled.

Daisy and I drank tea and talked. I asked if she knew anyone on the San Lorenzo Valley Water Board; and she told me about Archie Baxter, a board member, car salesman and retired army engineer, who had drawn up a proposal to build a dam downstream from her house in order to collect water in times of drought. Mac had been furious because a dam would expose the houses closest to the river to possible flooding. Mac said he would die before he would vote for such a crazy idea.

Shivers ran down my spine as I mentally put Archie at the top of my list of murder suspects.

Daisy looked up at the ceiling for a moment and drew in a deep breath, saying she didn't know the names of any other board members.

I felt like I was asking too many questions and Daisy looked tired. It was time to leave. But we agreed to get together for tea again. As we hugged each other, she winced and said goodbye.

I stopped in the doorway.

"I hope I didn't hurt you, Daisy. Paul said you have a few health issues…."

"Just some arthritis; doesn't everyone?" she chuckled, and closed the door.

Solow padded out to the truck, and I hoisted him into his seat.

Our four-block drive ended at the curb in front of the Ben Lomond public park across the street from Park Theater. It was twelve-thirty and some children were entering the building while others were leaving, but most had food and drink in hand. Tabatha, Kate and Gypsy crossed the street and sat down at the table I had already claimed. Their lunches were homemade. I told myself I should have been prepared and brought a lunch.

"Josephine, what are you doing here on your day off?" Tab said.

"I had a visit with Daisy. She's a very nice lady."

Tabatha nodded. "Yes, she is."

"Have you heard of Archie Baxter?" I asked no one in particular.

"I know him," Kate said, as she adjusted Gypsy's sling. "Archie sells cars in Santa Cruz; he's the caretaker of the Park Theater, and he's on the water board, right?"

"Right, and he wants to build a dam over Mac's dead body."

"Seriously?" Kate said.

"That's how it sounded coming from Daisy." My stomach growled as I watched Gypsy suck on a cold drumstick dipped in soy sauce. "I wonder if other board members want a dam built."

"The only way I can see having a dam," Kate said, "is if it's built here, by the park where the original dam used to be. Even then, it would have to be taken down before winter every year."

I noticed a familiar white Ford 150 pickup roll into town and turn at the Ben Lomond Market parking lot. I excused myself, clipped a leash to Solow's collar and we crossed the street just in time to greet Ben as he slid out of his seat and slammed the door.

"Ben, how's it going?"

"Hey, Josephine, I see ya got that good ole dog with you."

"I figure Solow and Sara are kinda like dog cousins." We stood for a minute leaning up against the hot metal of his shiny white truck. "Ben, do you know anyone on the SLV Water Board?"

He rubbed his white whiskered chin for a moment. "Well, there was Mac…and there's a guy named Blue Stone—Indian fella from Arizona. He's here to save everything that creeps, crawls or swims.

"Where does Blue stand on the dam issue?"

"He doesn't believe in dams but he's big on ladders, you know, fish ladders." Ben's blue eyes wandered across the parking lot to the store and back. "Does that help ya? I know you're working on Mac's murder," he smiled wickedly.

"Yep, that's what I'm doing, and yes you have helped. Thanks, Ben. Give my love to Aunt Clara."

"You got it, Josephine." We hugged goodbye.

I watched Ben as he marched over to the market entrance, admiring his tall straight physique, easy stride and long grey ponytail swishing back and forth from under his Giants cap—not bad for a man in his mid-seventies.

Solow tugged on his leash. I followed his lead, straight to a fire hydrant painted yellow. When it was properly anointed, we crossed the street looking for Kate. The picnic tables were all empty. Obviously she had finished her lunch and taken Gypsy and Tab back to the theater.

As I stepped into the street for another crossing, a souped up red and white motorcycle with a sidecar screeched its brakes, swerving and fishtailing halfway around, and back to the direction it came from.

In his rearview mirror, the young rider and his sidecar girlfriend probably saw my gob-struck demeanor as it morphed into seething rage. Breathing in burnt tire smoke, I picked myself up from the street and looked around for Solow. Like an arrow, he shot down the middle of the road, through a red light and out of sight. My only thought was, "What if his leash catches on something?"

How fast can a basset bounce on short springy legs? Surely he wouldn't go far. But I changed my mind when I remembered finding him at the old hotel, three miles up the mountain.

Quickly I ran for my truck, climbed in and took off for Daisy's neighborhood. I caught the next red light, waited for green and stepped on the gas—only to have to stop for pedestrians. I was beyond antsy. Finally I made it to Daisy's, and pulled the truck to a stop behind a boxy white mail truck. The mailman had his arm in Daisy's mailbox.

I jumped down from my seat and ran to the front door as the little white mail truck moved on to the next property.

The dogs voiced their interest, and Daisy opened the door.

Before I could say a word, she said, "He was here a moment ago, but, he took off that way." She pointed to the other side of the street.

"Thanks, Daisy. Mind if I leave the truck here?"

Before she had time to answer, I was across the street, climbing a steep set of brick stairs that led to a house set back from the road about a hundred yards. I circled a tool shed and dodged garbage cans and children's outdoor toys, calling Solow the whole time.

No howling, no answer, so I put myself in high gear and began climbing the mulchy mountain.

Chapter 9

For young adults, mountain climbing was once a great pastime, that is, before the current electronics craze came along. For me, hiking was necessary, something I had to do in order to find Solow. He and I were a team. I fed, walked and bathed him. He made me happy in a hundred different ways, sometimes making me laugh until tears ran down my legs.

After the first stretch of forest, I quit calling Solow. Instead I focused all my hopes, strength and breath on getting to Paul's place. I thought about the abandoned hotel. Did it have a name? I didn't remember seeing any signs or mention from Paul as to what the name of the place was.

After about twenty minutes of powering up the mountain, legs burning like Roman candles, I plopped down on a fallen redwood for a quick rest. As I sat gulping air, I felt something on my leg and brushed it off. It was a centipede. I looked closer at the decaying tree bark and discovered a world of tiny critters. Where the tree rested on leaf-covered earth, odd-looking mushrooms grew.

A blue jay squawked. I jumped. Another jay answered his friend. And then the forest was quiet again.

I stood up and set my flip flops in motion, up hill, always up until I finally found a section of the logging road heading south. Soon, it angled north, then back to south. And so it went.

The quiet mountain had grown even quieter as all valley noise ceased. I felt like a tiny helpless bug caught in a giant terrarium.

Thinking back several hours, I had dressed myself in a tank top, shorts and flip flops, thinking I would simply be casually dropping in on a few people to ask questions about Mac's murder. Even in Aromas, Thursday morning had been extra sunny and warm, so naturally I dressed for the heat. Actual shoes would have helped get me through the forest, and Levis would have kept the prickles and poison oak off my legs. But life happens and for a second time, I was ill prepared to tackle the mountain as I searched for my wayward basset.

I put a hand in my short's pocket to make sure my truck key was still there. It was there.

Finally the logging road leveled, just before it swung up to the right. But there was a choice. Not far ahead, a flat, level, beautiful pathway beckoned on my right. Dozens of palm trees stood at attention, soaking up filtered sunlight, circled and dwarfed by giant redwoods. My heart and mind floated into the Land of Oz. Soon I would have Solow. I called his name over and over as I strolled toward the hotel.

The iron gate complained loudly when I opened it. Looking around the front yard scramble of rose bushes and tall weeds, I discovered something new, water gurgling into the fishpond. A frog croaked from the rock formation circling the Monet-type water feature.

What if I came all this way and Solow wasn't here?

Suddenly I felt something cold and wet touch the back of my bare leg. Twirling around, I was relieved to find Solow at my feet. I looked up, up and there was Paul holding the end of the leash.

"I hope you don't mind, Josephine. I've been teaching Solow some walking etiquette."

Kneeling down on the ground, hugging Solow, I had no words. I just smiled a lot.

"He's resistant to change, but he did pretty well today," Paul said.

I stood up. "I see you filled the pond…."

"So many projects here…I'm never bored. Would you like to see my garden?"

"Sure, as long as it doesn't involve anymore hiking or climbing." We laughed as we headed around the building to the back yard. Solow walked like a gentleman at my side, no pulling or lagging and no detours.

"Looks like these beds are ready for plants…oh, something's coming up already." As I looked around, I realized that dozens of tiny leaves were breaking through the dirt in nice even rows.

"That one's spearmint, this is thyme and that's coriander. There's a bunch more that haven't come up yet," he said.

"Will you be using them to spice up your food?" I asked with my limited knowledge on the subject.

"Some of them. Mostly I'm experimenting with different compounds to control and possibly alleviate pain and disease. It's a hobby of mine…."

"That's some hobby!"

"Between you and me, Josephine, I want to pay back Daisy for all the years she sacrificed her time and interests so that she could give me a good education. She's a good mom and a good teacher. Every time I go down to the house to pick up food, she has more books set out for me to take." His crystal blue eyes looked moist.

"I understand that Daisy has seizures and arthritis," I said, "but what can you do about it?"

Paul smiled. "Never stop trying to heal her."

"And what are you growing over here besides mushrooms?"

"Just mushrooms. I'm a bit of an expert on them. I've found dozens of varieties growing in the forest…."

"Aren't you afraid they'll be poisonous?" I asked.

Paul shook his head. "Nope, been studying and eating them for years. I know I'm only seventeen, but don't forget, I was home-schooled. Daisy taught me how to find information instead of playing kick-ball on the playground. I know something about the world, even though I didn't see it for myself, just on TV and the computer," he chuckled. "I even have a cell phone. Daisy charges it up whenever I leave it at the house."

"So how do you get your food, books and phone without anyone seeing you, like Tab and Al?"

"Easy, there's an outside door to the basement and I have the key. I used to live down there. Let's just say it wasn't Daisy's idea. But it worked for me. I like to be alone—mostly, and I usually travel at night."

"And you like to be barefoot…."

"Yeah, and good thing because they don't make shoes my size," Paul laughed. He walked away from the herbal garden to show me the rotting stump of a pear tree and pointed out four old living pear trees that had grown up from fallen fruit. He guessed they were about four generations away from the original stump. The evidence was all around us, twisted, crusty, leafless trunks and limbs of fruit trees, and here and there a young tree bearing fruit.

Even though I was known by my friends and family as the worst gardener on the planet, I suddenly realized the potential of this Garden of Eden with its filtered sun, pure water and mulchy earth. Even without caretakers for the last century, the backyard garden had survived. And with Paul's help, I was sure it would thrive.

"Paul, where did you get your horticultural experience…."

"I learned from books and film—and Daisy, of course. Daisy let me grow things in pots around the house, and I had a grow light in the basement. But I didn't get much hands-on experience because I wasn't allowed to go outside in the daytime.

"Because Mac didn't want anyone to know you existed…."

"Yeah, but since I only sleep five hours or less every night, I was usually up around two or three o'clock, roaming the mountains until the sun came up."

"What about cougars and…."

Paul rolled his eyes. "I'm bigger than a cougar and that's the biggest animal in this forest. Besides, I have a way with animals," he grinned, looking directly at Solow. "My girls, the German Shepherds, take turns sleeping. One is always awake in case Daisy has a seizure or falls for any reason. Anything happens, one girl is out the doggy door and at the fire department in less than two minutes. The other girl stays with Daisy. I sure miss those girls."

"What are their names?"

"Willow's the darker one wearing the lavender collar and Wanda wears the green collar. Everyone just calls them, The Girls."

I kept Solow on his leash as we said goodbye to Paul and made our way down the logging road, through the neighborhood and across the street to Daisy's place. I had mixed feelings about Paul being sequestered in the old hotel. Was Paul ever lonely? Would he spend his whole life up there?

I tapped on the front door and Tabatha opened it.

The girls burst out the door to greet their newest club member. Solow stood in the glow of their affection and peed on the mailbox post. It had been a perfect day for him, exhausting for me. Tab took one look at me and invited me in for a glass of lemonade. The dogs followed us inside, through the living room, dining room, kitchen and sliding glass door to the deck. It was late afternoon and the sun had already fallen behind the western mountain range.

I walked up behind Daisy lounging on a chaise with her feet up.

"Hi, Daisy…."

She snorted loudly, looked around with blinking eyes and saw me. "My goodness, you're here again?"

"I just came by to let you know that I found Solow…ah, up in the hills."

Daisy looked at me for a better explanation, but that was all I put forth. With Tabatha sitting next to me, I didn't think I should talk about Paul so I just sipped my lemonade.

Eventually Tabatha excused herself, saying she needed to go to her room and work on a song she had just learned.

Solow and the girls were sprawled on the deck catching a few winks.

Daisy watched Tab enter the house. "Did you see him?" she asked.

"Yes, I did. He's growing herbs and mushrooms, and he taught Solow how to walk like a gentleman on leash. He's amazing."

"I know. I miss him." She stared at a plastic bracelet on her wrist.

"Why don't you ask him to come back? Mac's gone, and I think Paul has a lot of self-confidence. I think he would be fine…."

"Josephine, do you know that he is still growing? There are many layers to Paul. He has special abilities some people won't understand, and he has a hair problem…has to wear long sleeves and long pants to cover it."

"You talk about him like he's some kind of Big-foot creature…."

"I just try to see him as other people would see him." She twisted the bracelet around her thick wrist until the word, "Diabetic" appeared on top.

"Daisy, I saw a nice young man with tons of brains and good manners. He's cheerful, thoughtful, ambitious…what more could you want from him?"

"Thank you for your opinion, Josephine, but I'll have to think about it." She stood and walked me through the house and out the front door. The girls followed us outside and indulged in one last Solow sniff before I hoisted him into his seat. He fell asleep immediately, curled up in a ball, probably dreaming about Paul and his girls.

Driving south, back to Aromas, I wondered why Daisy would be worried about the layers that made up a boy named Paul.

Chapter 10

Friday morning Solow and I marched into Park Theater at nine o'clock sharp, just a minute before Alicia and Trigger arrived. A large group of children sat on the floor in the middle of the room singing their "good morning" song. Kate walked through the doorway with Gypsy tied to her chest. She saw Trigger and immediately asked him if he wanted to join the circle of singers. He politely nodded and joined the group.

Solow settled down under a worktable while Alicia and I discussed what we would paint that day. Communication was tough since the carpenters were cutting wood and pounding nails in the alley.

Janinne motioned to me from the other side of the room.

I quickly made my way around the circle of singing children.

Janinne leaned closer, "Josephine, would you please ask Frank and George to keep the door closed as much as possible?"

I nodded and retraced my steps back to Alicia and Kate who were discussing colors to be used on the pirate ship. Squinting from the change in light, I entered the sunny side alley and found Frank, the shorter more muscular of the two men, cutting a piece of plywood into an intricate design with a jigsaw while long, tall George shortened two-by-twos with a band saw.

"Hey, you guys, try to keep the door closed, okay?"

They didn't look up, but George nodded his head of distinguished-looking premature grey hair.

I reentered the main room, closed the door behind me and found Alicia in the backroom organizing her paints. I loaded my palette and picked out a couple of good brushes.

Alicia left the room.

The wooden staircase beckoned. The yellow crime tape was gone so I climbed the creaky steps, opened the door and stepped inside the attic. Already the fifteen-foot by fifty-foot room was plenty warm.

Layers of painted props and piles of stuffed animals leaned against the long wall ahead of me. The wall behind me provided storage for a huge collection of hardware, mostly lighting equipment and boxed light bulbs stacked on metal shelving. Off to my left were odd pieces of furniture, chairs, stools and small tables. To my right, two long rows of hanging costumes sweltered, and to the right of the door stood a wooden bench painted white. On the floor in front of the bench were yellow chalk marks.

I looked away. My heart raced and sweat dripped from my brow. The heat was getting to me, or was it the knowledge that Mac had died in this very room, probably on that old peeling white bench?

It was time to get back to painting scenery. As I stood on the landing, I checked out the door locks. Over time, three locks had been installed. The top one was a simple latch, below it was a lock requiring a key and below that dangled a simple metal hook. I gave the attic door an extra push to make sure it was wide open. With each downward step, I felt the temperature drop. Finally on terra firma, I grabbed my palette and brushes and began Friday's work.

Painting a pirate ship out on the bay kept me on my toes, constantly comparing my painting with the printed picture Kate had given me. She said another larger ship was coming, once Frank and George finished cutting out all the pieces. The cabin, with its ornate pirate decorations, would be painted on the wall. Everything below the cabin would be three dimensional and made out of wood, supporting various platforms for the singers and actors doing their "Yo-ho-ho" routines.

At the stroke of one, Alicia, Trigger and I took a lunch break in the park with Solow and three Mountain Man sandwiches. I had just tossed our little bag of dirty napkins, paper cups, straws and raw onion slices into the trash barrel, when I looked up and saw Daisy and The Girls crossing the street. Prancing side-by-side, the beautiful German Shepherds wagged their tails to Solow's delight.

Daisy flopped down on our picnic bench and let out a big sigh. Even though she was only in her early fifties, she looked like she had not one drop of energy left, not one more step. She waved a hand at the dogs, a signal that they were allowed to roam the park until she decided to call them back. Our three tail-waggers took off across a concrete basketball court.

Alicia said she wanted to go back to the theater and finish painting sails on one of the ships in the harbor. Trigger left with his mother, explaining that Kate had a job for him.

I turned to Daisy. "How are you getting along, now that Mac is…gone?"

"I'm fine…okay, I guess. My sister pays me well to take care of her children." I detected a chill in her voice. "She never wanted children, but she knew I wanted them. I'm tempted to introduce Paul to Albert and Tabatha…."

"They would be cousins, of a sort, don't you think?"

"I hope so," the volume of her voice fell below the river's gurgling.

Keeping the conversation going, I described Paul's garden and the delicious spring water he served to me in a paper cup. I told her about things like a chicken-wire platform where herbs and mushrooms dried in the sun, and described the orchard where pears and apples grew on the descendants of hundred-year-old fruit trees.

Daisy mentioned the medicine Paul had compounded using herbs and other natural ingredients. The cream took away her pain and the tinctures helped her to keep her blood sugar in the "safe zone." She told me about her unfortunate history with doctors who prescribed medicines that she was allergic to.

I needed to get back to work but wondered how Daisy would be able to walk the four blocks back to her house since parts of it were uphill. When I asked her about it, she said she would sit on the bench until her energy came back.

"Daisy, let me give you a ride home…okay?"

"I didn't mean to interrupt your work, Josephine, but I would appreciate a ride home. You're a dear." Daisy pursed her lips and produced a dainty whistle. Instantly The Girls turned to look at her. She waved her little hand and all three came running. By the time Daisy trudged over to my truck, I had three dogs in the bed expecting a ride.

I left the snug top in its open position since the springs were strong and the ride would be short and slow.

Daisy looked at their happy faces and giggled. "Three Whiskateers. I don't think The Girls have ever ridden in the back of a pickup truck before," she said, settling into her seat.

I turned the key and slowly pulled away from the curb. "Solow always rides in the cab, so this ride is very exciting for him." I braked gently at a yellow light and crossed the intersection with a green one. We rolled along into an old shady neighborhood.

One block from Daisy's house, a siren erupted behind us.

And then I saw the flashing red light and the blue light in my side mirror.

"Must be for someone else," I said. Then I remembered I had three dogs in the back. I knew there was a law against driving with unsecured animals in the back of a pickup truck—but it was only a few blocks. What could happen? My cheeks felt hot as I tugged the steering wheel to the right and parked in the weeds. A minute later, Sergeant Smothers introduced himself to me and said, "Howdy Mrs. Mackie."

"How's the investigation going?" she asked the sergeant.

"We've decided it was an accident. Somebody probably locked the door not knowing anyone was inside."

Was Daisy upset or relieved? I couldn't tell.

"How often do they lock the attic?" I asked.

Smothers gave me a cold, black-eyed stare. "Not sure, ma'am."

"You never asked that question?"

"No, ma'am; did you?"

"No, but I will…."

"Let it go, ma'am, and I'll forget your citation," he grinned. His straight white teeth, smooth brown skin, deep voice and smug attitude didn't impress me. The man acted like he was God's gift to women, causing my hackles to go up and stay up.

"It's okay, Josephine," Daisy said. "I can accept that it was an accident."

"Okay, ladies, guess that's settled. Have a nice day." He handed me his card, and turned back to his vehicle.

"He hasn't seen the last of me," I grumbled under my breath, tossing his card on the floor. I checked the rearview mirror. Smothers waited for me to pull out first, so I complied. One block later, I parked in front of the Mackie mailbox.

The Sheriff's green and white SUV swished by and disappeared around the next turn.

I turned to Daisy. "That guy is one of the investigators of Mac's murder…?"

Beep-beep, someone tooted a horn behind us. I looked around to see if it was another sheriff. Nope, but the mailman looked short-tempered as he drummed his thumbs on the steering wheel, waiting for me to pull away from Daisy's official federal mailbox. I drove the truck forward twenty feet, shut it down and asked Daisy a second time if the sheriff was working on Mac's case.

"He's the only investigator," she said as she opened the passenger door and dropped her short legs into tall weeds.

Together we off-loaded the dogs, and I slammed the snug top shut. "So he determines whether there's a case for murder or not?"

"That's right, but I'm ready for it to be over. I need to move on," she said.

The Girls watched Solow pee on the mailbox post, then one at a time did their best to raise a leg.

The mailman snapped the mailbox shut, and then his little mail truck lurched forward into traffic.

"Daisy, would it be okay with you if I take a look at Paul's room in the basement?"

"I suppose it would be all right, dear. You'll need the key." She pulled her keys out of her purse with shaky hands, peeled off one key from the ring and handed it to me.

"I'm going inside and lie down for a few minutes," she said.

The Girls bumped the front door open for Daisy, followed her inside and nosed the door shut with a snap of the head.

Solow and I veered off to the right, down a narrow concrete path leading to the lower back of the house. We came to a discrete side door painted the same shade of brown as the exterior of the house. It was the door to a basement room nestled under the deck.

The neighborhood was quiet except for gurgling, splashing noises coming from the river, the occasional squawk from a blue jay and the slam of a basement door when I pulled it too hard. Staring into the darkness, I waited for my eyes to adjust. When they did, I searched the walls for a light switch. There were no switches because there were no light fixtures, only one small lamp on a desktop.

I stumbled around various pieces of furniture for about fifteen feet, working my way to the other side of the room where a tiny bit of light filtered through a small curtained window. When I pushed aside the heavy fabric, a tiny amount of light made its way through lush greenery outside. Some light was better than none.

Laughing to myself, I sized up Paul's narrow bed. It was made out of two-by-fours and plywood, and it was eight feet long if it was an inch. Someone had made a thin mattress from scratch and covered it with an eight-foot length of foam rubber and a set of homemade sheets.

Looking around, I discovered a computer, a small TV, a radio, a box of test tubes, a filing cabinet, a desk, two chairs and a dresser full of XX tall long sleeve shirts and pants.

To my left was a door. I peeked inside. The little room had a shower stall, a toilet and a small mirror touching the ceiling above the sink. Nothing fancy, just serviceable. How could Paul have lived here in the gloom for twelve years and come out with such a chipper attitude?

Just for fun, I flipped through Paul's filing cabinet. I pulled out one file folder titled, "Daisy." The recorded information began six years ago when Paul was only eleven. His handwritten notes were very astute as he documented her pain, blood sugar levels, behavior, temperature and PH levels. A chart showed Daisy's gradual improvement. Feeling like I was snooping where I didn't belong, I glanced quickly through the paperwork, then stuffed it back into the file cabinet.

I checked my watch. It was almost three. Tabatha might arrive home at anytime and discover me and the secret bedroom. Again I reminded myself that I needed to get back to work. Deciding not to wake Daisy, I dropped the key to Paul's room into my purse, loaded Solow into the truck and took off for Park Theater.

The theater air registered in the high nineties, bringing on instant perspiration. As I sidled up to Alicia to see how the old ship was coming along, she stopped her brush mid-stroke. "Where in the devil have you been?" she hissed. "I've been so worried…."

"Don't worry about me, I'm fine…."

"I'm not worried about my friend, the congenital snoop. I'm worried about Tabatha. She said she would meet me here after lunch and help us paint. Two hours ago she went to the back room to find a better brush, one with a point, and I haven't seen her since. I told Kate and she said she hadn't seen her either."

"I'll look around," I said as I headed for the back room, like a squirrel running to water with its tail on fire.

Chapter 11

Ben Lomond's Park Theater had warmed up to one notch below intolerable. It was late Friday afternoon and most of the children had gone home, except for a few "stars" who stayed to work on their solos. Their songs and recorded music floated all the way to the back room where I discovered what was probably Tabatha's palette full of dried paint sitting on the counter near the sink.

A dreadful thought had brought me to that room. My heart pounded as I forced myself to look up to the top of the stairs. Charging up the staircase, two steps at a time with my eyes on the door, I screamed, "Help, help!" all the way to the landing.

Alicia, Trigger, Kate and Frank came running and gathered at the bottom of the stairs, not understanding what all the shouting was about.

I flipped the ancient lock on the door up to the unlocked position and threw the door open wide. There on the bench was Tabatha, stretched out with her eyes closed.

Ugly yellow chalk lines still on the floor.

Frank came up behind me. "Call 911," he shouted to the folks standing around in the back room.

"Okay," Alicia yelled back. "Trigger, stay down here with me."

I held my hand to Tabatha's hot red neck, where I felt a fast, but weak pulse.

Frank scooped her up in his arms and quickly carried her downstairs.

I followed on shaky legs, cold sweat dripping down my back.

Boots pounded across the theater, up to the stage and into the back room. Two EMTs had run a block and a half from the Ben Lomond Firehouse, followed by sirens from a fire truck. The sirens quit and two more firemen sprinted across the wood floor carrying a stretcher and satchel of medical equipment.

Alicia, Kate and Frank stepped back to the stage area so the professionals could do their work. I was the last to leave the back room because I thought I saw Tabatha's eyes flutter.

Another siren and then silence. Everyone migrated to the front door. An ambulance stopped at the curb and Tab was loaded into it, ready for a twenty-minute ride to Dominican Hospital in Santa Cruz.

Albert arrived as the ambulance was leaving. He said he heard the sirens and ran from the market over to the theater to see what had happened. A couple of grocery clerks had followed him. Everyone wanted to know who was on the stretcher.

"Now, Al," Kate said softly, "it's Tabatha and she's going to be all right. It looks like heatstroke."

Everyone stood on the sidewalk staring at the ambulance as it ran a red light, careened around the corner and raced up Highway Nine, lights and sirens fully engaged.

"But how…?" Al whimpered.

"Someone locked her in the attic," I said.

"Same as Mac," Kate said, wrapping her arms around Gypsy. The little girl quietly studied the worried faces around her, then smiled at her favorite friend, Trigger.

"Are you okay, Allie?" I asked

"Yeah, I'm okay, but Trigger will be staying home with his father from now on."

"I don't blame you. It's getting scary around here." I shivered as a gust of wind ruffled my wet shirt.

We entered the theater, but our work seemed unimportant. All we wanted to do was comfort each other and be comforted. Kate was obviously distraught because she was the one who had asked Tabatha to find a particular pirate costume in the attic and bring it to her. Kate said she had asked Tab to go because her ankles were swollen and she didn't want to climb the stairs carrying Gypsy who was teething and had been unhappy most of the day.

I looked around for Frank and checked the alley—no one there. The guys must have called it a day. Maybe I should too, after all, it was four-thirty. I called Aunt Clara to make sure they were home. She told me she was shelling peas and Ben had a pork roast slow cooking on the barbecue. I was practically drooling at the thought and told her I would be there in about an hour.

Alicia had already cleaned her brushes and tidied up the sink. Trigger, the "old soul" of the group, hugged me and told me not to worry, and off they went in the family station wagon.

Albert told me he was going straight home.

Solow stood at the entrance door wagging his tail—a hint to me that we should go. Kate was right behind us and the last to leave. She locked the door and padded down the sidewalk to her minivan.

A siren bellowed as a Sheriff's car roared down Highway Nine, made the turn into town and stopped in front of the theater. The siren died and Sergeant Smothers climbed out of the cruiser.

Dang, one more minute and I would have been on my way to Aunt Clara's. "Are you here about the girl in the attic?" I asked.

"Yes, ma'am. Did you see what happened?" He pulled out his pad and pencil.

"I found her on the bench in the attic with the door locked, just like Mac."

"Pretty big coincidence," he admitted. "Everyone gone?"

"Yep, I'm the last to leave."

"How did you know she was there?" he asked.

"Just a feeling I had…." I watched him jot down my answer.

"You get those 'feelings' very often?"

"Not really."

He looked at me like I was the perp. "Anything you want to tell me?"

"I have no idea how it happened…."

"That's okay; I'll be back tomorrow. Don't leave town."

"Can I go to my aunt's house in Boulder Creek?"

He rolled his eyes. "Just don't leave the county." Sergeant Smothers climbed into his vehicle and drove away.

I hiked Solow into the truck and we rolled through town, plus two blocks of rural Ben Lomond, and parked in front of the Mackie house. One little errand, and then we would go to Clara's house. The Girls greeted us when Daisy opened the door holding her purse and sweater, looking like she was going somewhere even though all her sails had run out of wind.

"I guess you heard…." I said.

"Yes, Josephine. Thank God you're here. I very much want to see Tab at the hospital. My neighbor just came from town and told me the news a minute ago. I need to see Tabatha in person. You can leave Solow here with The Girls."

Solow was already sparking those beautiful German Shepherds and didn't even notice that Daisy and I had left him behind.

Half an hour and tons of traffic later, we parked at Dominican Hospital and hurried inside. Daisy walked as fast as her little legs could take her, all the way to the back entrance, better known as the Emergency Entrance. At the first desk we came to, she asked directions. A friendly nurse trainee, wearing her frizzy hair in pigtails, pointed to a waiting room further down the hall. She took our names and said a doctor would contact us.

We no sooner took our seats than Albert arrived.

"How did you get here?" I asked.

"Hitchhiked. She's my sister," he said firmly, and sat down.

The silence was deafening. Finally I asked if anyone wanted something to drink.

"Coffee," Daisy said.

"Coffee," Al said.

So off I went to look for a coffee machine. When I came back with two hot coffees, Daisy was talking to a woman wearing scrubs, stethoscope and a badge that said she was Dr. Alnite. The doctor finished her news and rushed away.

I handed off the coffees and sat down. "How is she?"

Daisy patted her eyes with a hankie. "They want Tab to stay the night. Her vitals have stabilized, but she's very weak. The doctor thinks she'll be fine. She's just sleeping it off."

"I'm staying," Al said matter-of-factly.

"All right, dear, I'll ride home with Josephine…if that's all right with you…."

"No problem," I said.

It was seven by the time I dropped off Daisy, handed her the basement key and boosted Solow into the passenger seat of my truck. In no time, he and I were experiencing the woodsiness of Highway Nine and then Big Basin Highway. We turned left at Tinker and roared up the hills to "Clara's Nest," recently named.

Ben greeted us with barbecue tongs in hand.

Sara was there in an instant, licking me and loving Solow.

Clara came out of the house looking rosy cheeked in her multicolored muumuu and rubber flip flops. Her pure white hair was pinned to the top of her head, but wisps of it had broken loose and moved with the breeze. She carried a platter of pu pus to a new round picnic table with a Lazy Susan in the middle. Clara placed the platter on the Susan and our nibbling began, along with my explanation for being late to dinner.

"Josephine, who was in the theater when this awful thing happened to Tabatha?" Clara asked.

I thought for a moment. "Kate, Alicia, Trigger, Frank and about six or eight kids practicing their songs with Janinne. The music was pretty loud and probably drowned out Tabatha's cries for help."

"Someone else had to be in that building," Clara said.

"If someone else was there, I didn't see him or her. Why would someone want to hurt a sweet girl like Tab?" I felt a lump forming in my throat.

An hour later, the deviled eggs were gone along with the tempura vegetables and coconut shrimp; and the hummus with raw veggies was about to run out.

Clara and I decided to take the dogs for a walk before we got into the main meal.

Ben stayed to watch over the pork.

Heading west toward the red, orange and purple remains of a sunset, we shared the trail with Sara and Solow who ran ahead. The path constantly curved right and left, but always headed downward. We came to a small brook, kicked off our flip flops and stepped into six inches of cold water. After a minute or two, the water felt good.

"Do you and Ben come down here very often?"

"Are you kidding? We're always so busy. Ben installed a furnace last week. No more carrying wood and feeding the fires all winter," she laughed. "We're getting soft in our old age."

"No, just smart. Auntie do you know anyone on the SLV Water Board, other than Mac?"

"I'm pretty new around here, but Ben might know someone."

"I already talked to him about it. As you can imagine, I'm trying to put together a list of suspects. And now it's all twice as complicated."

"Is Mac's wife under suspicion?" Clara asked.

"Probably not, even though there are some things she put up with from Mac that most women wouldn't. Have you met Daisy?"

"No, I haven't, but I just adore Tabatha and Albert. We better head back to the house, dear, while we can still see the path."

The trail led us to a perfect dinner, but the murder's trail was as elusive as ever.

Chapter 12

Because July Fourth, Independence Day, was just two days away, holiday excitement was everywhere and especially tangible on children's faces. The Ben Lomond Firehouse was draped with red, white and blue bunting, Scarborough Lumber sported a row of large American flags waving from tall poles bordering the parking lot, and smaller flags made in Korea were posted all over town. Someone had pinned a small flag to the phone pole in front of Park Theater where I parked.

Aunt Clara and I clambered out of my truck and into the theater. It felt strange not to have Sara and Solow with us, but I wasn't about to let them ride in the back of the truck after my warning from Sergeant Smothers. Besides, Ben said he appreciated their company.

It was Saturday and I came to work with loads of energy after sleeping on a lovely bed in Clara's guest room. She had inspired Ben to turn their little cabin in the woods into a real home, room by room.

Frank walked up to me. "Josephine, you're looking much better today."

"Thanks, yesterday was not my best day," I said, pouring three shades of rusty brown onto my palette. "You looked a little weak in the knees yourself."

He groaned. "Not my best day either. How is Tabatha doing?"

"All I know is that she stayed overnight at the hospital. I see the yellow tape is back. See any sheriffs around?"

Frank looked up to the top of the stairs. "Haven't seen any."

"How often do they lock the attic door?" I asked.

"Only between plays when they rent the building out—you know, for private parties and stuff. Archie has the key. I need to rip out that useless bolt." Frank glared at the door, as sweat ran down his red face.

Alicia arrived in time to hear my brief report on Tabatha's condition and Frank's explanation about locking the attic. She hummed, "Yankee Doodle Dandy" as she prepared her palette and grabbed a couple of brushes. We began painting half a dozen very tall trees along the shore of the lagoon where a distant sailing ship was anchored. It was my favorite kind of painting—telling a story with pictures.

Kate suggested we add a few birds and some deer.

Kyle joined us an hour late, explaining his alarm hadn't gone off. His spiky red hair had been parted and combed to one side, and he had obviously left home without his usual earrings.

We three painters shouted back and forth over the sawing, hammering and loud western music, but finally gave up and slipped into our solitary painting modes. Several times I returned to the back room for one thing or another, and each time I stared at the door at the top of the stairs to make sure it stayed wide open.

I finished painting the tree I was working on, dropped my brush into a pot of water and decided to stretch my legs by walking from room to room. I walked the length of the back room, all the way to the boys' changing area and the girls' changing room and turned left into the "hallway tunnel" used by the actors to get on stage. As I felt my way along the unlit tube, I tripped on something and fell to my knees.

"Ouch!" I felt the floor with my hand. It felt like one board was slightly higher than the other boards. Feeling foolish, I stood up and continued my walk to the stage. Fortunately the last half of the tunnel was blessed with a bit of light coming from the stage area. I felt the walls for a light switch, but didn't find one.

As I turned around and tried walking the tunnel again, heading to the back room, three little boys ran through the hallway barely missing me. At the far end, I found a light of sorts, a long string hung from the ceiling. I tugged on it and a forty-watt bulb blossomed. The bulb dangled ten feet above the twenty-foot-long tunnel like one firefly over an acre of darkness. Some people might say it was spooky.

Doubling back to the middle of the tunnel, I tried to see what I had tripped on. Just like I thought, a floorboard was raised by a quarter of an inch, just enough for my flip flop to get caught. I ran my hand over the area and felt more uneven wood, a square of it.

The three little actors galloped through the tunnel as if I wasn't there. I stood up, walked back to the sink and searched through a bucket of brushes, remembering a beer bottle opener I had seen among the brushes. I clutched the rusty little item in my hand and hurried back to the tunnel. Music blared as I pried the uneven two-foot by two-foot section of wood up an inch, two inches, a foot. I looked down through the open hole into a possible basement devoid of light, and smelling of dirt and pine.

The three little boys appeared at the other end of the tunnel so I quickly slammed the trap door down, and stepped out of their way. This time Aunt Clara was right behind them. The boys turned, saw her, stopped short and returned to their stations.

It was almost lunchtime, too late to start painting another tree, so I moseyed over to where Kate was measuring a squirmy young man for an eye patch. I helped hold the little pirate still.

"Kate, does this theater have a basement?"

"Not that I know of…hold still, Brian…."

She jotted down the measurement, and I set the little pirate free.

Next I visited the carpenters working in the alley that separated the Ben Lomond Market from the Theater. The two men were sweating buckets under the southern exposure.

"Watch it, Josephine," Frank warned, as he turned a sheet of plywood over and began sanding. A few feet away George pounded nails into a portable set of stairs.

"Do you guys know if there's a basement in this building?" I shouted.

Frank shut down his sander and George stopped hammering.

"Is there a basement in this building?" I repeated.

Frank looked up at the blue sky for a moment. "Don't think so."

George chimed in with, "Nope."

"Thanks, guys." I turned and walked down the alley to the street, turned right and right again at the corner of the Theater. The two-story front facade was plaster, but the other three sides of the building wore wood siding. From the front corner to the back of the building I closely examined the North wall, looking for irregularities of any kind. As I moved along, bent over with my butt in the air pushing weeds out of the way, someone tooted a horn behind me. Expecting to see a fresh kid in a sports car, I looked around and laughed when I saw Kate driving her minivan, waving.

She pulled to the curb and shouted, "Lose something?"

"Just my flip flop," I said, holding up my shoe for her to see.

Kate laughed and roared away.

Even though I was on the shady side of the building, my cheeks felt hot. Kate must have thought I was crazy, creeping along in the weeds like a mad dog.

When I reached the back end of the North wall, I looked up at the wooden siding of the theater, all the way up to the attic, a sad reminder of the room at the top. I rounded the building and continued my search along the eastern side. At the end of that wall, I turned around and double checked the backside again.

Something caught my eye. A broken, dried up branch was lying in the weeds. A wild lilac bush stood in my way so I pushed on a stiff branch until it snapped and fell into the weeds. Kneeling down for a better look at the siding, I pushed on a board and discovered it was loose. I pulled on it hard. Two boards nailed together fell to the ground on their face, exposing two metal rings attached to the backside. The rings had obviously hung on the two hooks screwed into a support beam.

After estimating the size of the hole in the wall, I instinctively looked to see if anyone was around. An old woman happened to be walking along the sidewalk. I waited impatiently for her to climb into her compact car and drive away. The second she was gone I sat down and scooted feet first into the dark hole. I tried hard not to think about spiders as I slid down a six-foot dirt embankment and landed on flat sandy dirt.

Looking back at the hole, I wondered if I would be able to climb out if necessary. Dust glinted and swirled around an army of thick wooden pillars holding up the first floor of the theater. Naturally the basement was dark and smelled of old wood, but the dominant odor was fresh new pine.

Thinking back to the trapdoor in the tunnel overhead, I counted off twenty paces across the earthen floor, as cool silky sand sifted between my toes. Suddenly my shoulder smacked into a five-foot-high wooden structure built out of rough pine two-by-fours and four-by-fours. The freestanding staircase was attached to nothing, and ended about four feet below the basement ceiling.

After a moment of deliberation, I put one foot on the first step. The structure didn't wobble so I tried the second step. As I reached the fourth step, the top of my head touched the ceiling. The fifth step was a small platform just big enough for me to balance on my knees. Logic told me the trapdoor would be directly over the platform.

Reaching up, I ran my hand along the beams overhead. Feeling nothing unusual, I decided I would just push on the wood directly overhead as hard as I could. The wood moved under my pressure. Very quickly I had an opening big enough to hoist myself through. But the hoisting took every ounce of upper arm strength I could muster.

Once I was in the hallway, I lowered the trapdoor and sat on the floor breathing hard.

Three little actors ran through the tunnel, barely missing me.

Aunt Clara caught up to the children and told them to go get their lunch boxes and meet her outside on the sidewalk. She saw me pulling myself up from the floor.

"Josephine, what happened to you?" Her eyes traveled from my mussy hair down to my filthy feet and flip flops. "Your knees are all scratched up…."

"I know, remind me to tell you all about it when we get back to your place tonight."

"That's fine, dear. Right now I need to gather up all the children and walk them across the street to the park. Are you and your friends going to have lunch over there?"

"I haven't talked to them about it, but I think we'll see you over there, Auntie."

After more quizzical looks from Alicia and Kyle, I told them I had simply gone outside to get some air and lost one of my flip flops in the weeds. Alicia rolled her eyes, Kyle shrugged and off we went to the market to buy our lunches. Once we had our food, we joined Aunt Clara at her picnic table.

Kate pulled up at the curb, climbed out of her car and unstrapped Gypsy from her seat. They joined us at our table while a dozen little actors ate their lunches, crammed together six to a bench at another table. Kyle looked torn between a table full of women, a table of children and the table next to us where Frank, George and several teenage volunteers wolfed down their Mountain Man sandwiches. In the end, he chose our table.

"Like, what goes on here on the Forth of July?" Kyle asked Kate.

Gypsy sucked on a piece of crust from her mother's sandwich.

Kate answered with, "Ben Lomond locals typically attend the Boulder Creek Parade in the morning and the Scotts Valley Fireworks Show at night. We decorate all over Ben Lomond and there's a pancake breakfast at the firehouse."

"Hey, look whose coming," I said.

We watched Albert angle across the street, straight to our table.

"Hi, ah, I didn't go to work today," he said, "like, I told my boss what happened to Tabatha, and I didn't get fired. They even gave me today off so I could take care of her. I just wanted to thank you guys for helping my sister yesterday." Albert's voice cracked as he looked at me and then Frank. "She's home now," he said over his shoulder as he hurried away in the direction of home.

A sense of relief washed over me. But a moment later, I worried about Tabatha all over again because we still didn't know who locked her in the attic or why. But at least I knew how a person could get inside the theater without being seen. Suddenly I remembered leaving the "door" to the basement open.

After lunch I headed for the back of the theater instead of going inside. Leaning down, taking a last look into the basement, I watched as three little boys scampered up the pine steps and climbed through the trap door into the theater. "Good grief!" I said to myself, as I quickly closed the entrance door to the basement.

Chapter 13

Saturday afternoon was not as hot as Friday and relatively uneventful, allowing us to paint the animals and birds Kate imagined. At four in the afternoon Alicia said she needed to leave so that she would have time to shop for groceries.

I asked Aunt Clara if she was ready to go home.

"I couldn't be more ready…" she said, looking out of sorts after a day of trying to herd a bunch of third-graders into a fitting of pirate costumes she had been sewing.

"Would you mind if we stop at Daisy's house to see how Tabs doing?" I asked.

"That's a lovely idea, Josephine."

We settled into the cab of my pickup for a four-block ride. Minutes later I parked the truck in front of Daisy's house, behind a sheriff's green and white cruiser, and helped Clara out of her seat.

Daisy opened the front door. The Girls greeted us with energetic tail wagging. I introduced Aunt Clara to the lady of the house but before we could step inside, Sergeant Smothers and a taller younger sheriff with blue eyes and sandy blond hair walked up behind Daisy. Apparently the two men had finished their business and were leaving.

I followed the deputies over to their official sheriff's car. Smothers saw me coming.

"Now that Tabatha was almost killed, has your investigation resumed?" I asked the Sergeant.

"As a matter of fact we're working on it," Smothers said. "Deputy Wolfe, this is Josephine…."

"Stuart," I added. "Have you found anything new…?"

"I'm afraid I can't discuss that with you," the sergeant said. He slammed his door, fired up the engine, did an illegal U-turn and headed into downtown Ben Lomond.

"And if *I* find anything new, I'll keep it to myself," I said to myself. I opened the front door and walked in to find Clara doting over The Girls. Daisy asked us to come out to the back deck for glasses of lemonade. We gratefully accepted the invitation and followed her through the house to where Tabatha was curled up asleep on a chaise lounge. Daisy leaned down and whispered something to her. She slowly opened her eyes, raised her head and looked around.

"Hello, Tabatha, how are you feeling?" I asked.

"Okay, just a little tired," she yawned. "The doctor told me to get lots of rest."

"Do you remember anything that happened in the attic yesterday?"

"It was so hot up there. I found the things Kate wanted, and I remember hearing someone coming up the stairs. There was a sweaty odor and I heard a floorboard squeak. But you know how loud the music is, so I might have imagined it."

"Anything else?"

"The door slammed shut. I tried the doorknob, it turned, but the door wouldn't open and pretty soon I was yelling my head off but no one came. My head hurt and it just got hotter and hotter. That's all I remember."

Albert came pounding up the back stairs onto the deck. He stopped short, looking surprised to see us. "Ah, hi…."

"Al dear, would you mind picking some lemons for the lemonade I promised everyone?" Daisy said, dropping into a chair next to me.

Albert scampered back down the steep flight of stairs and came back minutes later with at least a dozen lemons cradled in his t-shirt. He carried them to the kitchen, juiced them and when the tall drinks were served, I asked where the lemon tree was located. Tabatha walked me over to the deck railing and pointed down to the top of a large, fully loaded lemon tree.

No wonder Paul's room was so dark. Even if Paul opened the curtain on his one little window, most of the light was already blocked by the lemon tree.

Aunt Clara joined us at the rail. "What a lovely tree."

"Yes," Daisy said. "I can smell the blossoms from the kitchen."

I was dying to talk to Daisy alone. Finally I asked her to show me where the bathroom was. She looked puzzled at first but took me into the house and down the hall. I noticed there were no pictures of Paul anywhere, and wondered if anyone had ever taken a picture of him. He wasn't even close to good looking, but he had an infectious smile and Daisy obviously loved him very much.

We stood in the hallway and talked about Paul in hushed voices. I told Daisy about the lovely old hotel where he was living and all the renovating he was doing. She told me about Paul's love of animals and his high intellect. She said she was still putting out food for him every night, telling Tabatha and Albert the food was for the raccoons. When I asked Daisy if she would let Paul come home to live, she looked at the floor and shook her head.

"Daisy, do you mind my asking what the sheriffs were doing here?"

"Of course not; they said they have a lead…a rumor about a very tall person who was spotted in the area the night Mac died, and they think the same person locked the door on Tabatha." She shivered. "They wanted to know where I was Saturday."

"So you and the 'tall person' are suspects," I gasped. "Or are you the get-away driver?"

Daisy laughed. "I explained to the Sheriff that I had a dental emergency the day Mac went missing. I don't drive much. Nerves," she chuckled. "Mac and Al weren't home so I called Archie for a ride. Dr. Spicer saw me around one o'clock and it was three by the time I got home. You see, Dr. Spicer's office is across the street and two doors down from the theater, so of course I was seen near the murder scene."

She continued, "I remember feeling a bit fuzzy when I stepped outside the office. I don't like to be without The Girls, and Archie had taken them for a walk. Dr. Spicer took my arm and helped me over to Archie's car. I should have been helping him to his car. He's pretty old and rickety," she snickered.

"Did Officer Smothers tell you anything else?"

"Well, he said that some tools are missing from the theater and he wanted to know if Albert is interested in carpentry. I said I didn't know. He's only lived here for two weeks," she frowned.

"The man doesn't have a clue!" I snarked.

Walking through the house to the deck, we both came down with the giggles.

"What's so funny?" Clara asked.

"The sheriffs think Daisy is a person of interest."

"Ridiculous!" Clara stammered. "What kind of detectives have they got around here?"

"They're both easy on the eyes," I said, "but I'm not sure how well their brains are working."

"Don't worry, Daisy, Josephine is good at this sort of thing," Clara said with a sly smile. "She'll find whoever locked Mac and Tabatha in the attic."

Actually, I knew that Aunt Clara was pretty good at collecting clues too. "I guess Tabatha is the only one above suspicion," I mused. Daisy had just placed Archie at the scene of the crime, along with a host of volunteers.

"Are you ready to go, dear?" Clara asked me.

"Huh? Oh sure." I nodded, and said goodbye to Daisy, Tabatha, Albert and The Girls.

As we climbed into our seats, my phone began ringing. It was Ben wanting to talk to Clara. I handed her my phone. We were almost to Boulder Creek by the time she put the phone back in my purse. She said Ben wanted to have dinner at Scopazzi's Restaurant and asked us to meet him there.

We were definitely not dressed for eating out but did it anyway. I parked the truck and we walked a short distance, veering to the right of Scopazzi's entrance, over to the outdoor dining on the deck where Ben sat with friends.

Ben, David and George all stood up and pulled chairs for us. Ben hugged Clara, David hugged me and George introduced us to Kit Malone from Texas. He didn't have to tell us she was from Texas because Texas was in every word she uttered. She wore her long straight black hair pulled to one side, her checkered skirt short and a giant engagement ring on a long slender finger. I looked down at my naked ring finger, wishing I was dressed up for dinner and wearing the diamond ring David had given me.

A waiter arrived and took our orders.

It was eight o'clock and Clara and I were starving.

"Ben," I said, "how do you know George?"

"I just met him tonight. The way I understand it, George works with Ernie Quintana at the University and they both play golf with David. Small world! Too bad we didn't get Ernie and Alicia over here."

"How did you all get together, anyway…?" I asked.

"It was like this, Ben and I came down here about an hour ago," David said. "And there was George and his beautiful intended. Sorry, George, no intimate dining for you guys tonight," he laughed. "So we've been having a great time shootin' the bull, and waiting for you."

Kit's eyes looked tired. She sipped her wine and the guys ordered specialty crafted beers. The chitchat continued until dinner was served. After dinner Clara, Kit and I traipsed together through the restaurant to the powder room.

Kit walked up to the mirror, pulled a tissue out of her beaded purse and scrubbed at the smeared mascara under her brown eyes.

"I hate when that happens," I said. "Are you okay?"

"Yeah, I guess. It's not the first time. George just doesn't get it."

"Get what?" Clara asked.

Kit held up her ringed finger. "He feels more obligation toward his momma than he'll ever feel for me."

"Maybe he needs more time." I thought about the last ten years of David courting me. "Some things can't be hurried."

"I'll hurry that boy whether he likes it or not," she growled.

Feeling sorry for Kit, I pulled a business card out of my purse and handed it to her. "Call me if you need someone to talk to."

"Well, thank you kindly, Josephine. I just might do that."

By the time the three of us arrived back at our table, the stars were coming out and I was feeling chilly and out-of-place in my shorts and flip flops. On top of all that, although I loved my Auntie dearly, I wished I were going home with David.

Kit and George said their goodbyes and drove away in a sporty red Camaro.

Clara looked even worse than I felt and she couldn't stop yawning. It had been a long day for both of us. Ben helped her into his truck and headed up the Big Basin Highway. I followed them in my pickup, taking comfort in remembering David's parting kiss.

I parked behind Ben's truck and watched the newlyweds enter the house.

My phone rang.

"Hey, Josie, I just wanted to warn you not to go into that stupid attic at the theater," David said. "George told us what happened to Tabatha yesterday."

"Don't worry, sweetheart, I'm not going up there. I snooped around the theater a bit today and found a secret entrance...."

"Josie, honey, you're at it again. Why do you think you have to solve every murder that comes along?"

"I haven't solved it; I just wanted to know if there was a way to get into the theater without being seen...."

"What else have you discovered?"

"That Daisy is a person of interest to the police. Is that crazy or what? And even crazier, the sheriff sounds like he thinks Al is stealing tools from the theater."

"You're right, Josie, that's crazy. Mac was a big strong guy and Daisy's a little bitty lady. Maybe Mac's son from Minnesota came to California and did it," he laughed.

"What son...nobody told me the Mackies have a son living in Minnesota...." I gulped.

"The way Mac phrased it, the kid must be his son from a former marriage. Mac golfed with us a few times and this one time he was bragging to Ernie, George and me about how smart his kid is and how the kid made a serum that's been helping Daisy to get well. He swears she's a good eighty percent better. Even her doctor says so."

"Her arthritis or her seizures or her diabetes?" I asked.

"Cancer."

"You're kidding!"

"Nope."

Chapter 14

Sunday morning I woke up to utter silence, except for a wall clock ticking in the kitchen three rooms away. Solow slept peacefully. Being used to Clara's noisy energy flying through the house in the form of a vacuum cleaner or her beloved ukulele, I wondered if my seventy-five-year-old aunt had finally run out of gas.

I pulled on my robe and trundled down the hall to the kitchen where I found a note stuck to the toaster.

> Dear Josephine, I didn't have the heart to wake you. Since I am not needed at the theater until Monday, Ben and I are driving up to San Francisco for the day.
>
> Happy painting my dear!
>
> Clara

Solow wandered into the kitchen looking for breakfast.

"Okay, Solow, this means Aunt Clara is fine and you're going to the theater with me today. You would look great in a tux, but we're going casual this time."

After a quick shower, I slipped into ratty but clean paint shorts and a paint-smeared t-shirt. I cooked up a great omelet and shared it with my buddy. When it came to culinary delights, Solow was my biggest fan. Everyone else knew my cooking as either over, or under-done and sometimes worse than that. Stored in the back of my mind was an image of David wearing an apron as he carried a fabulous meal to the table, while I lit the candles. It was clear to me that we would have to iron out a few details once we were married, like his house or mine for starters and who lights the candles.

Solow howled with excitement from his passenger seat window as my little red Mazda flew south on Big Basin Highway onto Highway Nine and eventually pulled to a stop at the curb in front of the Ben Lomond Theater. I tooted the horn when Kate opened the entrance door. She turned and walked up to Solow's window. Gypsy, Kate's semi-permanent appendage, squealed with delight as Solow gave her chin a lick.

Kate stepped around the front of the truck and stuck her head in my window. "There's something I need to tell you, Josephine. Remember the three little wild pirates running around here Friday? Well, one of them confessed to his mother that he locked the attic door…."

"Oh my gosh!" I murmured. "That changes everything. Mac's murderer didn't harm Tabatha after all."

Kate smiled, "A little cooler today, don't you think?" as Gypsy cooed over the roar of Kyle's motorcycle.

"Yeah, I think it is a bit cooler." I smiled. "There's Alicia across the street, and here comes Kyle." I helped Solow down to the sidewalk.

Kate stepped closer. "I talked with Janinne and Frank yesterday. They think our painters are doing a great job. The three of you are invited to the appreciation barbecue this coming Wednesday afternoon at two. It's for the volunteers, but you can bring a friend if you like," she winked and smiled.

"Thanks, sounds like fun." I dreaded one more long drive to Ben Lomond, but the picnic tempted me.

"Next week we should be ready to paint the free-standing pirate ship the guys are putting together," Kate said, as we entered the theater. Her voice faded away, cut off by the sawing and hammering noises coming from the alley.

I quickly closed the side door. "Kate," I said, "Frank seems like a quiet guy. Is he always like that? And where was he the day Mac died?"

"I see where you're going with that…you heard about the fight he had with Mac…."

"No, I didn't hear about a fight. What happened?"

Alicia walked closer. "What fight?"

"Yeah, what fight?" Kyle echoed.

"I'll tell you at lunch. We need to get started," Kate said.

On bouncy legs, Solow headed straight to his favorite under-table hideaway.

"What was that all about, Jo?" Alicia asked.

"I don't know yet. Kate knows something…."

Alicia shook her head slowly as we walked across the expanse of wood flooring, up five steps, across the stage and into the back room. I ignored her indifference to the Mac murder case, knowing I could never be "sensible" like my best friend.

My mental roster of suspicious people had just gained another name. I tried to imagine sturdily built Frank sliding into the basement and crawling up through the trap door to the first floor hallway. Sizing him up, at five-foot-ten and two-hundred pounds, he wasn't a likely candidate to have entered the building in such a way. Besides, the murderer could be anyone who normally worked in the building, including Kate, Janinne, George and half a dozen other volunteers. Realistically, I hoped Frank was innocent.

Before I gathered my paint supplies, I glanced up the stairs to the attic. Looking up there had become a habit.

As soon as Alicia and Kyle left the back room, I took the stairs to the top and stood for a moment on the landing. I moved the latch up and down. It moved with very little pressure.

The temperature rose a few degrees as I entered the attic, even though it was only nine o'clock in the morning. Being a congenital snoop, I couldn't help searching the room for clues. Starting at the far left wall, I discovered that one of the chairs was missing a leg. Looking around the room, I found the missing leg near the door.

As I walked the fifty-foot-long west side wall, examining a variety of stored props, I laughed out loud when I saw an interesting little car made out of wood. It was large enough for two little kids to sit in, and it looked like the "Back to the Future" DeLorean. I pushed the car to see if it had moving parts. It rolled a few inches and hit the wall. I pulled on it and it rolled away from the wall, just enough for me to see a hinge. I picked up a tall fake palm tree and set it off to my right, exposing another hinge. Since hinges usually come with a door, I quickly dragged a stuffed gorilla away from the wall and proved my theory. Actually, the hokey "so-called-door" was made of the same white-painted wood as the walls around it.

I heard footsteps, shoved Mr. Gorilla back in front of the funky door and casually crossed the room to the top of the stairs where Kate stood breathing hard and Gypsy giggled.

"There you are, Josephine. Frank and George are ready to set up the ship and they need our help."

Kate and I thundered down the stairs and joined Alicia and Kyle on stage. The four of us held steady a twelve-foot-long, five-foot-high wood cutout of the bottom section of a sailing ship while Frank and George screwed the facade to various platforms specially built for young singers and actors. Once the ship was stable, we were free to go back to our work, or in my case, begin my day's work.

Alicia gave me the "look."

"What? I was just looking around up there."

"Where?"

"In the attic, of course," I said, as I painted long feathered leaves on a palm tree.

"Jo, do you think it would be okay if I stay home tomorrow with my family for the Fourth of July?"

"Allie, we can call the shots around here because they are so lucky to have us…."

"I wouldn't worry about it, Alicia," Kate said, walking up behind us. "Josephine's right, we're very lucky to have you painting for us. Enjoy the holiday tomorrow, both of you. Actually, you won't miss much. Frank, George and a couple of other guys plan to work here till noon tomorrow." She turned and walked away.

"Jo, your face is so red," Alicia laughed. "By the way, did you see the notice posted outside on the chain link fence…about a meeting of the Water Board, and the public is invited…concerning the drought?"

"No. When is it?"

"Today at five o'clock, in the library."

"Thanks, Allie, I'll be going to that."

Three hours later, we took our lunch break at the picnic tables. Allie, Kyle, Kate, Janinne and I ate our sandwiches while Solow babysat Gypsy in the sandbox. We shared our table with Frank and George because local teenagers had already taken over the other three tables. Albert was one of those teens. I watched him concentrate on his new friends, ignoring us completely.

Suddenly brakes squealed, a door slammed and a woman wearing short shorts, a tank top and four-inch heals marched straight to our table. Kit's arms flailed in the air as she approached her fiancé.

George put down his Mountain Man sandwich.

"Come on, George, yer Momma needs you," she said. "I think she might be die'n."

"Where is she?" George practically choked.

"I called an ambulance…" Kit said, grabbing his shirtsleeve. George squiggled his long legs out from under the table and the couple ran to the Camaro. Tires smoked and they were gone.

I looked at Frank. "Something wrong with George's mother?"

Frank shrugged, his face still beet red from the heat. "He never even said she was sick."

Our group went silent and stayed that way for many long minutes. We thought our thoughts, the teens played their music and the river shimmered under the midday sun. Beauty was there for the taking—if only life were that simple.

Alicia, Kyle and I sweated our way through three more hours of painting. My painters brushed white primer on the freestanding wooden part of the ship, plus one palm tree, while I painted George's new set of stairs to look like it was made out of rustic planks.

Around four thirty, Kyle left, explaining he had a date with Kelly.

Alicia drove home shortly after that.

It was almost five. I had just enough time to clean the brushes and scrub paint off my hands before the water board meeting started across the street at the library. I freshened my lipstick, ran a comb through my hair and walked Solow over to the library.

Standing in the doorway looking across the crowded room, lined on all sides with loaded bookshelves, I tried to size up the crowd. Straight ahead at the far side of the room, three men and a woman sat in swivel chairs behind an oval table. Obviously they were the "board members." Four rows of six chairs each were already filled with town folk.

I made myself comfortable leaning against the back wall with Solow lying at my feet.

A middle-aged man, dripping sweat into his frizzy grey beard, read the minutes from the last meeting and offered a moment of silence for poor departed Mac. I figured the bearded one was Archie because he looked at least a decade older than the other two men sitting at the table.

Shirley Logan was easy to spot, as was Mr. Stone with his shock of black hair. I couldn't identify the fourth board member.

The audience of locals booed at the suggestion of a rate hike and cheered when repair work on outdated water pipes along Zyante Road was proposed. Obviously the people were attending the meeting because they had strong feelings about some of the issues.

Archie executed the agenda in calm, somber tones, oblivious to the emotions of the audience. He never looked up and never missed a beat, even when he pulled a handkerchief from his pocket to wipe his brow.

The library's main room was the size of a typical grade school classroom and filled to capacity. Even with the door wide open, the room became stuffier by the minute.

One lanky young man arrived late and sidled up to me at the back wall.

"Albert, what are you doing here?" I whispered.

"Uncle Mac needs to be represented...."

"That's great, Albert; your uncle would be proud of you."

"Not really," he whispered. "Mac never liked me."

"Shhhh!" came from an elderly woman sitting in the back row.

The meeting droned on.

I yawned. My feet were unhappy. I leaned on one leg for a while then the other. An hour passed and half the crowd had left the building. Albert and I settled into folding chairs in the back row right after the crabby old woman shushed us for the last time and left.

Finally, Albert and I were the only audience the board had. I wondered if Archie had arranged the issues so that most people would have gone home by the time damming the San Lorenzo River came up for discussion.

Suddenly Solow began to heave, his back arched as he sent forth loud groans. Not wanting to disrupt the meeting, I quickly pulled him by his leash to the exit door. Once we were outside, just ten feet from the park, he coughed up three pieces of a June bug and remnants of a Mountain Man Sandwich.

I tied Solow's leash to a post and leaned my head in the doorway. I was able to hear most of Archie's plan for a dam plus disgruntled remarks from two of the other members. And then I listened to one brave teenager giving his uncle's side of the issue.

Chapter 15

Fourth of July was one of my favorite holidays. Even though Monday was not a paint day, I stayed Sunday night at Clara and Ben's house in Boulder Creek because I wanted to see the Boulder Creek parade early the next morning. I awoke thinking about the night before, watching Albert bravely stand up at the water board meeting and make a very good case for not damming the river. Too bad the town folk had already left.

I remembered how Archie seethed under the bright ceiling lights in the library's main room, while Blue Stone grinned and the other two members of the board kept their feelings to themselves. Were they afraid of their outspoken senior member, or did they not have opinions on the issue? If Mac was killed over his dam position, was Albert in danger? Probably not, since the boy was only sixteen.

***

Standing in Clara's shower stall, I went over my Fourth of July plans, which included a visit with Daisy after the parade. In the evening, I planned to watch the Watsonville fireworks show from Alicia's house, with David, of course. Solow would have to stay home. He never appreciated fireworks. In fact, they freaked him out. That's why we left Sara and Solow at the house while I drove Clara to the parade. There would be way too much noisy stimulation for our sweet, sensitive dogs.

Aunt Clara agreed it was a great parade, but the Firehouse Band was the best part of the small town entertainment. Dressed in lumberjack-style knitted caps, kilts and big yellow fireman boots, a couple of dozen fit and fine-looking volunteer firemen marched with enthusiasm behind ten firemen musicians pounding drums and tooting horns. Obviously the men had been practicing their routine for quite some time. Each man had grown a beard and learned the synchronized march that involved twirling fake pick axes over their heads and shaking their booty for the roaring crowd.

By noon the parade was finished and a million pieces of candy had been thrown from various floats and scooped up by kids dressed in red, white and blue who waved little American flags.

As we wove our way through the crowds toward my truck, Aunt Clara pointed to a painted pony being walked up the street to a vacant lot where the horse trailers were parked. The teenage girl walking the red, white and blue pony had painted white stars on a blue background covering the horse's hairy body, and ringed its legs with red and white stripes.

I turned my head to admire the pony, wondering what it would be like to paint on Solow's fur.

"Oh…sorry," I said, as I smacked into an oncoming pedestrian.

"No harm done. Did you enjoy the parade, Josephine, Clara?" Janinne asked.

"Absolutely! Do you watch the parade every year?" Clara said.

"Every year…my husband's a volunteer fireman," she laughed.

I tried to tell Janinne how much we enjoyed watching the firemen, but the crowd pushed her up the sidewalk as Aunt Clara and I were being pushed in the other direction. An antique store beckoned and Clara pulled me through the doorway. I didn't have the passion for antiques that my aunt had, or a budget for such things, but looking was fun and gave us something to do until the sidewalk traffic thinned out.

I drove Clara home, collected my suitcase and Solow and drove south, halfway through the San Lorenzo Valley to Daisy's house. As Solow and I climbed out of the truck and walked up to the open front door, a heavenly bacon smell emanated from the kitchen.

Daisy invited me to join her for lunch.

The Girls welcomed Solow by sniffing him up, down and sideways with girlish vigor.

We found Tabatha at the stove frying bacon. She greeted me with a smile. "You'll stay?" she said.

"I wouldn't miss it." I followed Daisy to the kitchen table and sat down. She looked more tired and pale than usual. "Is everything okay, Daisy?"

She leaned in my direction. "My medicine has run out," she said softly as the bacon spat and sputtered, and the stove fan whirred.

"Paul's medicine?" I whispered.

She nodded. Her face and hands looked puffy. "I'm a little worried about him. I put food out last night and it's still there."

Tabatha turned off the stove and the noisy fan, made three beautiful BLT sandwiches and poured iced tea into three tall glasses.

"I have good news for you, Tabatha," I said. "One of the little actors at the theater accidentally locked the attic door. He confessed it to his mother, and Kate told me."

"Wow, thanks for telling me, Josephine. I've been having nightmares. I was thinking the killer did it."

"That is good news," Daisy smiled.

"Where's Albert?" I asked. "I hope he didn't have to work today. Did he tell you he went to the Water Board meeting last night?"

Daisy nodded. "He told me he was there with you."

"That's right, but did he tell you he stood up for Mac's argument against the dam?"

"Oh my." Daisy put her sandwich down and pressed both hands to her heart. "He is a fine boy, isn't he?"

"You bet he is," I said, taking another bite of my delicious bacon, lettuce and tomato sandwich.

"He made some new friends," Tabatha said, "and they have all kinds of fireworks…."

Daisy looked down at her plate. "I hope they're the safe and sane type of fireworks."

"Anything else would be against the law," I said.

Tabatha rolled her eyes.

My cell phone rang. I excused myself from the table, went to my purse in the living room and answered the phone. It was David wanting to know what time I would be home and would I like to go out to dinner before we watched fireworks at the Quintana's house. I assured him I would be home in plenty of time to go to dinner.

Back in the kitchen Tabatha was finishing her sandwich, but most of Daisy's BLT sat on her plate. She had taken a few bites and gone to bed.

"Daisy isn't feeling well, is she?"

"No, my aunt has a lot of ups and downs, but she's been down for two days now and I'm worried…."

"I'll go talk to her. Maybe there's something I can do." I walked down the hall until I found the bedroom with Daisy in it. She looked so tiny in her king-size bed, curled up and half asleep.

"Daisy…Daisy…it's me, Josephine…."

"Yes, my dear, what can I do for you?" she sighed.

"No, it's what can I do for you? How can we get you some medicine?"

She ignored my question. "I'm worried about Paul. If only I could get food to him. I've been thinking about inviting him back to the house to meet his cousins. Al and Tab are such lovely people. They would be kind to Paul, I'm sure of it."

"That's a great idea, how can we contact him?"

"He has a cell phone, but it's in my basement being charged."

"If Paul doesn't show up tonight, call me and I'll climb the mountain tomorrow and see what's going on. By the way, do you know where Archie lives?"

"I'm not sure of the house number, but it's a two-story grey house with white trim on Dove Creek Road. Just go to the end of my street, turn right on Highway Nine, go one block and then right onto Dove Creek. You can't miss it."

"I'm going to leave now; is there anything I can do for you before I leave?"

"Don't be silly, Josephine. I have Tabatha here with me." As soon as her eyes closed, I went back to the kitchen. Tabatha handed me a zip lock bag with half a dozen homemade peanut butter cookies in it. I thanked her, and she said she would look in on Daisy later.

With the help of fresh cookie smell coming from my purse, I pried my basset away from his harem and helped him into the passenger seat of the truck. We cruised through the neighborhood and over to Dove Creek Road.

After a couple of miles of narrow two-lane windy road cutting through a heavily forested area, I finally spotted a two-story grey house with white trim perched on a cliff, half hidden by redwoods. I slowed the truck and gawked at a light blue compact Chevy parked in a carport below the house at street level. The backup lights were on.

I continued driving until I came to another driveway and was able to turn the truck around. By the time I got back to Archie's place, the little blue car was a quarter of a mile down the road. I caught up, but kept about ten car lengths distance between us.

Solow turned his long body to the open window and then back to my purse with cookies in it, then back to the window and over to the purse again.

"Okay, big guy, I'll get you a cookie." I fished around in my purse with my right hand and drove with the left.

Solow pressed his snout against my wrist.

"Just a minute…" I looked up. "Oh no!"

I slammed on the brakes.

Solow flew into the dash and rolled onto the floor.

Archie had suddenly stopped his car, just missing a family of skunks crossing the road. My truck slid right up to his bumper and tapped it before it came to a full stop.

So many things went through my head. Would Archie feign whiplash? Did he have a bad temper? Did he kill Mac over a stupid dam project?

First I checked to see that Solow wasn't hurt. He wasn't. He already had his nose in my purse again. I grabbed my purse and climbed out of the truck.

Essence of burnt rubber filled the air.

Archie stood with hands on hips examining the back of his car.

"I'm so sorry…." I said, looking down at the little dent in Archie's bumper.

He looked me over like he had seen me before. "Do I know you?"

"Not really, but I listened to you speak at the meeting last night."

"That must be it. Name's Archie," he said, holding a hand out for a handshake.

I hesitated but decided to trust him since he didn't know me from anybody. His crushing grip left me biting my lip. Solow must have sensed my pain and howled until I let him out of the truck.

"Hey, nice dog ya got there," he said, ignoring the dent in his bumper. "Some kinda hound dog?"

"Basset."

He nodded knowingly. "Well, nice meetin' ya…."

"Archie," I said. "Do you want my insurance information?"

"Heck no, the boss won't even notice that little bitty dent. I sell new and used cars and this little puddle-jumper is what the boss lets me use to get around in, old as the hills, but reliable. Sure glad I didn't get skunk all over it."

Archie hopped in his car and drove away.

Feeling grateful that Solow and I weren't harmed and the man didn't make a big fuss over a little dent, I started the engine and drove a few feet to the side of the road. I needed a minute to de-stress. The cookies helped. Even Solow settled down with the help of a cookie. I thought good thoughts like, how nice it was for Tabatha to bake for her aunt and give me some of the cookies. And then my mind wandered back to the concern on Daisy's face when she said Paul hadn't picked up the food she'd set out for him.

We left Ben Lomond and headed south to Aromas. The windows were down, and the radio was turned up as Julio and Willie Nelson sang, "To All the Girls I've Loved Before." Solow's ears flapped in the wind and my heart went piddy-paddy with the music as we traveled the length of Santa Cruz County once again.

My little house looked so welcoming as tires crunched up the driveway after three nights away from home. Sweet, thoughtful David had collected my newspapers and mail, piling them on the first step leading to the loft.

I checked my very old-fashioned message machine. It blinked red, indicating there were two messages. The first was from David telling me he would pick me up at seven for dinner. The second was from Tabatha. Between sobs, she explained that Albert had been taken in for questioning by the police.

Chapter 16

David picked me up at seven. Our reservation was for seven-thirty at the California Grill on Green Valley Road. We arrived in time for a glass of wine at the bar before dinner.

"Josie. Wine? Really?"

"Really," I said.

He ordered two glasses of white wine and asked me what was wrong. Should I give him the whole list, starting with Paul missing, down to Albert being taken in for questioning? I decided to compromise and share half of what I knew.

"I had a message from Tabatha, Daisy's niece. She was crying when she told me that her brother was a person of interest in the murder of their Uncle Mac."

"Sweetheart, I can see that you're upset. But if the kid did it, you'll have to let it go. You can't save the whole world…."

"No, I can't save the world, but I sure will try to save Albert. He's a very sweet, courageous, hardworking teenager. The world needs more kids like him." I took another sip of wine and felt my shoulders relax a bit. "Too bad his parents aren't around to see what a good guy he is. Poor Daisy has her hands full…."

David cocked his head. "What's going on with their aunt?"

"Poor Daisy, she's close to my age—just a couple of years older, but she's not in the best of health. She lost her husband about ten days ago. Her sister dumped her two kids on Daisy, but Daisy adores Albert and Tab. Her son's missing…."

"I thought you said her nephew was taken in for questioning?"

"Oh, did I say son? I meant to say that Albert was taken away for questioning." I took another sip of wine. "This will be so hard on her. I wonder how much more Daisy can take."

The very efficient greeter found us at the bar and led us across the dining room to a table by the windows. I settled into my chair and looked out the window at holiday traffic below, families and couples out having fun. I looked at David's reflection in the glass. A look of concern had spread across his handsome face.

Consciously putting on a happier demeanor, I changed the subject. "What have you been up to while I've been painting in Ben Lomond? Clara sends her love, by the way."

"Let's see…I finished picking apricots, think I'll take out a couple of the older trees. The old ones didn't produce much this year so I thought I would plant a few apple trees, you know, the kind where they graft limbs and you get four or five kinds of apples on one tree."

"How interesting." I smiled.

"Josie, you don't have to try so hard to look happy…."

"But I am happy and I love being with you."

"Sometimes I think you're not really here…."

"Sorry, David, I'm here now, and its time to order."

Dustin, our favorite waiter, took our orders. The food was served, we ate and talked and suddenly two hours had gone by leaving us just ten minutes to drive across town to Alicia's house before the fireworks started at nine-thirty.

David curbed the Miata close to the Quintana house. As we exited the car, the first bursts of fireworks popped, peeled open and rained down in spectacular beauty. We circumvented the house, using the side gate, and went right to the back yard where Ernie's mother greeted us with warm hugs.

Trigger and Tansy galloped across the lawn toward us.

"Grandma's watching me," Trigger said, "because Mommy slipped on Tansy's throw up in the kitchen and Daddy had to take her to the hospital."

Mrs. Quintana nodded gravely. "Dios mio."

"Tansy couldn't help it," Trigger continued. "She ate too much grass. Mommy said if I ate grass, I would probably do the same thing. She wasn't mad at Tansy at all." He bent down and the little sheltie leaped into his arms.

"That's too bad your mommy fell, Trigger," I said.

"Yes, ees very too bad," his grandmother agreed. She opened her mouth to say something else, but a series of loud pops, explosions and a rainbow of color had us all craning our necks and holding our breath.

As the crow flies, we were only a mile from the airport where the fireworks display originated. We heard smaller sizzles and explosions going off all around the neighborhood, but the big ones mirrored in lake water were the best.

Between loud pops and bursts, I asked Ernie's mother if Alicia broke any bones. She thought not but she said Ernie wanted to know for sure. Alicia had landed on her left wrist pretty hard. The kitchen floor being ceramic tile didn't help.

Mrs. Quintana, David and I relaxed on lawn chairs while Trigger and Tansy played ball. Trigger threw the ball a million times and Tansy retrieved it a million times.

When the fireworks finally ended with a spectacular grand finale, I looked around for Trigger. He and Tansy were curled up together in a wicker chair, eyes closed. Mrs. Quintana was asleep in her chair, head back, mouth open. I didn't have the heart to wake her. Neither did David.

We didn't feel comfortable leaving, so I found two lap blankets in the house and draped them on grandmother and grandson. Summer nights in Watsonville can be cool. That one was no exception. David and I went into the house to watch a movie on TV.

An hour later David went outside to check on our sleeping host and hostess. He reported they seemed to be down for the night. That was the last report I remembered hearing.

Suddenly lights were on and people were talking. Where was I?

"Josephine, you can wake up and go home now," Alicia said.

"Thanks for taking care of Mom and Trigger," Ernie smiled.

"Oh, they're outside…."

"No, Josie, they came in a while ago and went to bed," David assured me.

Alicia showed me the brace on her wrist, explaining that the whole emergency room and x-ray procedure had taken forever because of all the fireworks accidents, burns, etc. And after all that time waiting to be seen, the wrist was just sprained, not broken.

By that time, Ernie had melted like ice cream at room temperature. Wearing a five o'clock shadow and a few worry lines, he walked us to the door, yawned and said goodnight. I checked my watch. It was one o'clock in the morning; no wonder Ernie looked so tired.

I asked David if he wanted me to drive. He insisted he was fine and would do the driving. I turned my head to look at him, making sure it was David and not my father. They were so alike. Everything I loved and admired in Dad, I found in David. I felt like the luckiest girl in the world as my head pressed against the headrest. David pulled the Miata away from the curb and my eyes closed.

Next thing I knew, David was shaking my shoulder asking me to wake up. He gave me a hand.

I stepped gingerly onto loose gravel. My ankles wobbled side to side as my three-inch heels sunk with each step. But David's arm was steady—just like Dad's. He opened the front door for me and Solow shot past us, straight to a wooden gnome in my garden of withering flowers. He quickly anointed the little guy and darted back inside.

My sleepy fog lifted. I asked David if he would like something to eat or drink before he went home. With a sly smile, he put his arms around my waist and kissed my ear. We walked to the kitchen to look for a snack. On the way, I pressed the play button on my message machine.

"Who's that?" David asked.

"Shhh, I need to hear this."

David unwrapped his arms from my waist and sat down at the kitchen table.

I leaned down and poked the repeat button on the answering machine.

"I don't know what to do," Daisy wailed. "When I put food out for Paul, I noticed the basement door was open a crack. I called for him but there was no answer. Then I saw a crowbar in the path and gouges in the doorframe. It's a terrible mess in Pauly's room. What should I do? Please call me. I won't be able to sleep at all tonight."

When Daisy finished, David said, "Does the woman have a dog named Paul?"

"That was Daisy, Mac's wife, and Paul is their adopted son."

"Well, Josie, I thought I knew Mac and Daisy pretty well, but I never knew they had an adopted a son. I was under the impression Mac had a son back east…."

"They adopted him twelve years ago. Maybe they forgot to tell you."

"That's a big item to forget…."

"You have no idea…I mean, it's not a big deal," I said. "Paul's grown up and living on his own now. But Daisy likes to keep his bedroom ready for him if he ever needs it."

"Josie, I can see that your mood has changed. I'll probably see you tomorrow, unless you're off somewhere chasing a murderer," he laughed.

"I just need to call Daisy and reassure her that everything will be okay. She's been nervous ever since Mac died. And like I told you, Albert was taken in for questioning…."

"And Albert is the nephew?"

I nodded. "He happened to be at the theater the night his Uncle Mac was killed."

"You're really into this stuff…again. I wouldn't want to be the guy who killed Mac with you on the loose," he grumped.

"Goodnight, David." I followed up with a passionate kiss on his unsmiling lips.

No sooner had the Miata headlights disappeared down the driveway than I dialed Daisy. She picked up on the second ring, answering with the same intensity as the message she left earlier. I had hoped she would have calmed down, but if anything she sounded more nervous, afraid and borderline hysterical.

"Daisy, calm down and tell me exactly what happened."

"Well, it was eleven o'clock because I had just finished watching the ten o'clock news. Al and Tab had gone to bed…."

"Wait a minute. Albert's home?"

"Yes, they took him to the station in Santa Cruz and asked all kinds of questions. They brought him home around eight o'clock and told him not to leave town. Poor Albert was too upset to eat his dinner and went straight to bed."

"Poor Albert," I said.

"So like I was saying, I put some leftover roast beef, asparagus and some of Tabatha's homemade cookies in containers—like I do every night, and put the containers in the wood box near Pauly's door," she sniffed.

"Daisy, hold it together, and tell me everything."

"Sorry, Josephine, I'm worried but I can't call the police. They already took Albert to the police station this afternoon. He said they questioned him because someone said they saw him at the theater late Saturday night, the night Mac died." More sobs.

"Did Al say who pointed the finger at him?" Archie crossed my mind. If you're going to kill someone over damming the river, why not get rid of the nephew too?

"Poor Albert, he has no idea who it was."

"At least he's home now. Tell me what happened when you put food out for Paul."

"Like I said, I put the food in the wood box and then I noticed Paul's door was slightly open. I called out to him, but no one answered. That's when I saw scrape marks around the lock and a crowbar lying on the ground. I was shaking so hard, my flashlight went every which way. I took some deep breaths and looked into Pauly's room. It was dark so I stood there in the doorway for a while listening. But I was so scared, all I could hear was my heart pounding. I just hurried back into the house and locked all the doors."

"We know Paul wasn't home," I said, thinking out loud. "The question is, who broke in, and why?"

"I'm sorry to worry you, Josephine…."

"Don't worry about it, Daisy. I can't sleep anyway. I'll be at your house in an hour and we'll wait for Paul together."

Chapter 17

Posting a brief letter of explanation is always easier than risking confrontation on the phone. A pink post-it note for David would explain my absence. I wanted to spend the day with my love, but I had urgent business in Ben Lomond. Solow followed me around the house as I changed my clothes and gathered my purse, sweater and a bottle of water. He must have sensed my frustration. Do I risk life and limb and climb the mountain to find Paul, or do I talk Daisy into getting help from the police?

It was three in the morning when Solow and I left Aromas, and it was almost four o'clock when my truck rolled to a stop behind Daisy's little Fiat in front of her house in Ben Lomond. Instead of going to her front door, I decided to check Paul's room first.

Solow sniffed his way down the path. Chirping crickets went silent as we shuffled along under a starry, moonless sky. Paul's door was closed. With my fingers, I felt the gouges and splinters around the lock.

Solow sniffed the bottom of the door, wagged his tail energetically and surprised me with a howl.

"Shh!" I grabbed his collar and looked around to see if any lights went on in the neighborhood.

The door stayed closed. The lock was smashed, so I opened the door a crack and peeked inside. The room was darker than the moonless night. My skin went all prickly when I heard something move in the dark.

Solow pushed his way inside and bounded across the room.

"Paul?" I whispered.

A pitifully dim light flickered on. From across the room, Paul motioned for me to come inside and shut the door.

"I see you're eating the dinner Daisy set out for you."

"Yeah, she's great. Would you mind going up to the house and letting her know I'm here? And be very quiet, we might have a visitor."

"What visitor?"

"I don't know, but obviously someone broke into my place and stole my files. Fortunately my newest formulas are up the mountain at my summer place," he grinned.

"I'll go right up and get Daisy, but what's that on your ankle?"

"I injured myself. Took me two days to get here," he grimaced, sitting on his bed, his leg propped up on a stool with a foot-long stick strapped to his leg with strips of cloth that looked like t-shirt material.

Solow licked Paul's hand and gladly accepted pats and petting from his friend.

I left Solow with Paul, crept out the door and up the path to the front of the house. The street was quiet and dark as I walked up to the front door. The Girls growled. I whispered through the door that it was me, and they stopped at the sound of my voice.

Daisy opened the front door a crack, saw me and quickly ushered me inside. Her pajamas were wrong side out and her hair was mashed down on one side, but she was wide awake at four in the morning. When I whispered to her that Paul was downstairs in his room, she reached for the couch and slid down in a heap.

"Daisy, are you okay?"

"Oh my, just a little dizzy. Let's go see Pauly." With a sudden burst of energy, she stood up, took a flashlight from her desk drawer and walked out the door, hanging onto my arm for support.

We left The Girls curled up in their beds.

All was dark and quiet, except for crickets and a car door closing. An engine started up somewhere down the street.

Daisy flashed the light on the path in front of our feet. We rounded the corner of the house and walked quietly down to Paul's room.

A car drove by.

Worried about Daisy's short fast breathing pattern as she pulled Paul's door open, I guided her into the dimly lit room and quickly closed the door behind us.

"Oh, Pauly, I've been so worried…what's wrong with your leg, dear?" Daisy stood beside him at the edge of the bed and put an arm over his shoulder. In a sitting position, he was still a head taller than she.

"It's nothing," he said. "Don't worry. I have some salve in the drawer over there. Can you reach it, Josephine?"

I nodded, reached up, pulled the whole drawer loose and carried it across the room to Paul. He picked through a dozen or more little jars, finally finding the one he wanted.

"Josephine, I need a clean cloth and a bowl of water. You can put the water in that bowl over there."

While I followed Paul's instructions, he unwrapped his bandage. Strips of cloth and a piece of wood fell to the floor. We saw the smear of dark red, almost black blood. I cringed and Daisy paled. Paul gave me more instructions, which I followed as if he were an acclaimed brain surgeon. I squirted five drops of oily liquid from a squeeze bottle into the cold water, swishing it around with the cloth, wrung out the cloth lightly, folding it in half and laying it over the dried blood.

Keeping his voice very low, Paul told us about his accident. Two days ago he had packed his backpack with packages of dried mushrooms and herbs and freshly made medicines for Daisy. He said he was leaving the hotel, when a section of the front porch suddenly collapsed under his weight. It had taken him all afternoon to pull his leg free of the splintered wood, and then climb upstairs to fetch a bottle of his homemade antiseptic pain cream. He had wrapped his lower leg with strips of cloth from an old shirt. Halfway down the mountain, he rewrapped it, adding the stick for support.

"Mom, your medicine's in my backpack over there," he said, pointing to the lump on his desktop.

"Thank you, Pauly," she choked out the words, wiped her eyes and picked up the pack. She pulled out a clear plastic bag full of dried mushrooms and several other bags containing various herbs. Setting the bags aside, she pulled two four-ounce jars of something and stuffed them in her pajama pocket.

"I'll have the rest of it for you tomorrow," he said. "I'm afraid I can't go back to the hotel right away…."

"No, Pauly, you obviously can't go. I want you to stay here. I miss you so much and I think it's time you met your cousins. You've grown into a fine young man and it's time you lived in the world, not one little room."

The silence that followed seemed long and deafening.

Solow rested his chin on Paul's other foot.

Finally Paul spoke, "You're very sweet, Mom, but I don't…."

"Now, Pauly, I know what's best for you. We'll take it a day at a time. First you'll meet your cousins."

Paul turned his head, and looked at me with weary eyes. "You can take the cloth off my leg now and wipe the blood away."

Again I followed his instructions. When the wound was clean, I applied salve from another one of his little jars, working the strong smelling stuff down through his thick body hair. The medicine must have stung, judging by the tightness of his jaw and the blinking of his eyes. When I was finished, Paul smiled and thanked me.

Daisy talked to her son as if he were a sleepy little five-year-old, telling him to lie down and take a nap. As soon as he had stretched out on his eight-foot bed, she asked me to walk her up to the house.

I opened the door and looked around. The first tinges of pink light were in the sky, and all was quiet.

Reluctantly, Solow left his mountain man friend and escorted us up the path to the front door. Once he was there, he gladly joined The Girls inside.

"Josephine, would you like to stay the night? I can get you a blanket."

"Thank you, Daisy. I'm exhausted."

She brought me a blanket, I curled up on the couch and that was the last thing I remembered.

Chapter 18

Solow's wet nose on my cheek brought me out of a crazy-about-David dream state. Blinking and stretching, I looked around, trying to remember why I was sleeping on Daisy's couch. Solow and The Girls watched me as I stretched, yawned and checked my watch.

"My stupid watch is broken. It says it's noon. How can that be…?" I looked up at Tabatha coming in the front door.

"Hi, Josephine; you must have been up late last night," she said with a twinkle in her eye.

"Yeah, were you up…I mean, did you hear anything last night?"

"No," she said, "but it was so weird, I dreamt there were people on the path outside my window. I couldn't see their faces, but I felt like I knew them."

"I was here last night with Solow. Maybe you heard us?"

"Maybe," she shrugged.

"Did you go somewhere today?" I asked.

"I was practicing my part at the theater this morning, but I decided to walk home for lunch."

"So what part did they give you?" I asked, as if I didn't know.

"The lead," she looked at the floor and laughed. "I'm Peter Pan."

I reached over and we high-fived.

"What are you going to do with all that beautiful hair…?"

"Cut it off." Her voice shrunk as she uttered the words.

"You don't really want to, do you?"

Tabatha shook her head. "No, but I love playing the part."

"Any chance you can be Petra or Pamela Pan?" I asked.

Tabatha laughed, "What a great idea. I'll run it by Janinne."

"Tab, I hope you're being careful...."

"It's okay, Josephine. I've made a couple of friends at the theater and Kate and Janinne are always around. I'll be fine. The little kid that locked me in the attic didn't know I was there. When he slammed the door the bolt fell into the lock position. He didn't mean any harm." She went to the kitchen to make her lunch. When I joined her there, I saw that she had made two sandwiches, and one of them was for me. We ate together at the kitchen table while her aunt slept on.

When I finished eating, I thanked Tab and told her I should be heading home.

"I hope you like your surprise," I said.

"What surprise?" She cocked her head.

"Daisy will tell you about it tonight when Albert's home. I'll see you at the theater Friday."

I called Solow away from his two sweethearts, piled him into the truck and cruised down to Highway Nine. Traffic was light until we connected onto Highway One. Rather than sit in traffic for hours, I decided to stop in and see if Mom and Dad were home. We cruised through downtown Santa Cruz and turned onto Walnut. I parked my truck at the curb behind Mom's Subaru, helped Solow down from his seat and rang the same old doorbell I had used as a child.

Mom answered the door looking like a fat-faced stranger. Her skin was blotchy-red except for the pasty smears of calamine lotion across her face, neck and arms.

"What happened to you? Is that…."

"Yes, it's poison oak," she said, looking disgusted. "Bob and I went for a drive up the coast Sunday. I needed a restroom and your dad was thirsty so we stopped at this funky little gas station near Half Moon Bay. Well, on my way to the restroom I noticed some guy burning a big pile of brush on the hillside nearby."

"Oh no," I gulped, "not poison oak!"

"The smoke was blowing toward the gas station. Just my luck. Where's the ocean breeze when ya need it? But I didn't think too much about the smoke until yesterday morning when I woke up itching. Now look at me! He must have had some poison oak in that burn pile, and you know how allergic I am."

"Oh, Mom, that's awful. Is there anything I can…oh, I know where I can probably get you some help. There's this guy in Ben Lomond who makes medicinal salves and creams and stuff. I'll see what I can get for you."

"Well, if it's not too much trouble…I'm certainly not going back to my doctor after the last episode."

"It's no trouble at all. I'll be back in a couple of hours."

Somehow Solow already knew we were leaving and waited at the front door for me. Because Mom was also allergic to fleas and hated the thought of rogue dog hairs on the floor, Solow had spent very little time in that house.

I reassured Mom again that I would be back with help but did not hug her goodbye. I could barely stand to look at her puffy, weepy, rashy skin.

She bravely blew me a kiss and went back inside the house.

Off we went to Ben Lomond for the second time in one day. Even worse, it was my day off from working in Ben Lomond. What was I thinking? I didn't even know if Paul had anything that would help Mom's case of poison oak.

Halfway to Ben Lomond we stopped at a gas station in Scotts Valley, and I filled the tank. Solow hung his head out the window, his tongue flapping in the hot air as though he needed a drink of water. I rounded the gas pumps and entered the little Stop & Shop. The gal at the counter smiled like she knew me. But I figured it was because that's what everybody does in little towns like Scotts Valley, until she spoke. I recognized her raspy voice immediately.

"Josephine, how's the painting going? I haven't been back to the theater since Friday." The perky lady's head of yellow curls bounced as she spoke.

"Yeah, ah, haven't seen you around…you sew costumes with Kate, right?" I had no clue what the woman's name was.

"Yep, I have two kids in the play this year. Isn't that new girl, Tabatha, something? Pushed my Britney right out of the lead. I guess somebody else doesn't like her, whoever locked her in the attic like that…."

Not wishing to hear more gossip, I paid for a bottle of water and left the building. I shared the water with Solow, half of it in his bowl, the other half down my parched throat. When we were finally satiated, I fired up the truck and merged into northbound traffic.

My phone rang. I ignored it, but planned to get back to it later.

Arriving at Daisy's place felt like a rerun, like I was spending way too much time in Ben Lomond. But when I thought about Mom's poison oak, I knew I had to at least try to find help for her. Rather than bother Daisy, I followed Solow down the path to the back of the house directly to Paul's basement door and tapped on it lightly.

Solow howled.

"Come in, Josephine." Paul raised himself up into a sitting position on his bed. "I thought you went home," he rubbed his eyes.

"I was going home but I stopped in Santa Cruz to see my folks…" I put both hands over my face for a moment until my mother's image faded from my eyes. When I felt in control again, I said, "My mom's allergic to poison oak…."

"Sounds like she gets it pretty bad?"

"Yeah, but last time she went to the doctor with it, the medicine took over a week to start working and it burned her skin. She's really miserable."

"Hand me the drawer." Paul pointed to the same drawer full of little jars I had presented to him earlier that morning. He quickly read the handwritten labels on each one until he came to the one he was looking for and handed it to me.

I opened the jar and sniffed the creamy concoction. The strong aroma reminded me of lemon, lavender and musky mushrooms. I must have looked confused.

"I use essential oils, mushrooms and other things from the forest, whipped up in a cream made from lemon peel."

"So, how do you get it creamy, like this?"

"My Bullet," he smiled, pointing to a small blender on the counter. "Daisy has always encouraged me. She taught me how to do research, and she does her best to supply me with everything I need. When I was twelve, I was into experimenting with animal behavior. Daisy gave me four hamsters in a cage for Christmas," he laughed. "I wrote a book about their habits and behavior."

"At age twelve, you wrote a book?" I looked around the room to see if I could spot it. One shelf under the window had at least a dozen thick manuscripts in binders.

"Drives me crazy…I have talent in some areas, but sometimes human nature eludes me." Paul scratched his head, then ran fingers through his hair trying to straighten it up.

"Yeah, I know what you mean," I said. "People are funny, but what are you concerned about?"

"Mac let me live here. He built this room himself…so that I wouldn't be underfoot, as he put it. And no matter what his shortcomings were, I need to learn to forgive…."

"Forgive the murderer or Mac? I don't understand," I said.

"Yeah, I'm pretty confused myself," he mumbled.

"Paul, you were at the theater the night Mac died. Did you see anyone there besides Al and Tabatha?"

"Actually, I stuck pretty close to the kids because I saw someone wearing a hoodie poking around behind the theater—doing a little dumpster diving. Probably harmless, but you never know."

"Besides the hoodie, what did he look like?"

"Dark clothes…that's all I remember. That was the same night I discovered someone had gone through my old files while I was gone, and one file was missing. Maybe I mislaid it. Have a seat, Josephine."

I sat down on the end of Paul's bed.

"Awwk!"

"Sorry, didn't think your feet went all the way to the end of the bed. How tall are you, anyway?"

He shrugged. "Guess I'll find out pretty soon. Daisy wants me to go upstairs tonight. I'm a little nervous…."

"Afraid to meet your cousins?"

"No, I'm afraid the ceiling isn't tall enough," he laughed.

"Duck when you go through doorways and just be yourself. Your cousins will love you. How much do I owe you for the cream?"

"I don't deal with money. If you want to pay someone, pay Daisy. She buys my supplies online," he said, his eyes at half-mast.

The minute I said goodbye, Paul put his head down on the pillow and closed his eyes.

On an impulse, I stepped closer to the headboard and put my hand on his forehead.

He opened his eyes.

"I think you have a fever…."

"No, it's okay, Josephine. I run hotter than other people. You folks run at 98 and I run at 102."

"Do you remember your parents and do you remember what they did for a living?" I asked, hoping to learn more about his family and his background.

"I kind of remember them. They taught me how to live in the forest, not in words, but with thoughts."

"Wow, like you read each other's thoughts?"

"Something like that," he sighed. "I was very close to them."

"I'm so sorry, Paul…thanks for the cream."

Solow and I left Paul and hiked up the path to Daisy's front door. As I stepped up to knock, she opened the door and stepped outside with The Girls at her side.

"Josephine, did you sleep well last night?" she asked, as she walked thirty feet across the front yard to her mailbox at the edge of the road. She pulled the little door down, scooped the mail out and turned toward the house.

"I slept very well, thank you. Paul gave me some medicine for my mother's poison oak rash, so I want to give you this." I handed her a couple of folded bills and left before she could say anything.

Solow and I were on the road again, but so was the whole world it seemed. My sweet basset was asleep even before we were out of the neighborhood. As I drove, my thoughts were all over the map, but eventually settled on Paul and the type of person he was. Actually, I had never met anyone like him. He was bigger, stronger, smarter and kinder than anyone I had ever known. He seemed much older and wiser than his seventeen years. I hoped he would keep those wonderful characteristics, because his abnormal qualities were even more obvious than his attributes.

When I arrived at the house on Walnut Avenue, Dad let us in. He whispered, "Leola's resting," and pointed to the couch where my mother was lying on her back with an icepack covering her face. Dad, Solow and I moved into the kitchen. I gave Dad the little jar of medicine and passed on the directions Paul had given me.

"Tell Mom to smooth on a thin coat. Wash it off and reapply three times a day. Two days should do it, maybe three."

"Two days? You gotta be kidding…."

"Really, Dad, that's what he said."

"Who said? Who is this doctor anyway?"

"Ah, his name is Paul…Doctor Paul Mackie."

Dad squinted, his head cocked to one side.

"Don't worry, Dad, it'll be fine. Let me know how she is tomorrow," I said, inching my way to the door. "Love you, Dad," and out the door we went. Solow was always happy to be on the road home.

Chapter 19

Wednesday morning arrived with a howl from Solow and a knock at the door. My mouthy basset led the way to the back door where David stood holding a couple of dozen roses from his garden. He had tied a fat yellow ribbon around the assorted white, red and pink buds. A little trail of blood ran down his wrist.

"David, you're so sweet. They're beautiful, but you're bleeding."

"It's nothing, fair damsel," he grinned, "I taketh a thorn for my fair lady." He handed me the bouquet and plugged his wound with a tissue.

Still wearing my old walkathon tee shirt and flannel pajama pants, I pulled a large vase from a lower kitchen cabinet, ran the faucet and dropped the bouquet into the water.

Glancing at the clock on the wall, I said, "I'm getting in the shower right now, and I'll be ready in half an hour." It was already nine-thirty and David and I had planned to have breakfast in Watsonville.

After my shower, makeup and some intense work corralling my wavy hair into a banana clip, David was back. He held me close and said he liked my new white summer dress, and he liked my hair when it smelled like lavender. Twenty minutes later, my hair was a shambles and I couldn't find the banana clip. When all the lovin' was over, my sweetheart and I were starving.

I quickly put myself back together again and slipped on my lovely engagement ring from David. We said goodbye to Solow and headed into Watsonville to the California Grill.

Dustin took us away from the greeter-lady and led us to a nice table in the far corner of the room where we quickly reviewed the familiar breakfast menu.

Dustin returned to our table, his pencil poised on a note pad.

David went with the eggs Benedict and I ordered the eggs on polenta dish. We sipped hot coffee and held hands across the table.

"Did you see the article about Ben Lomond in the paper today?" David asked. "Something about building a dam…."

"You mean they're actually going to build it?" My jaw dropped.

"They're putting it up for a vote in the next election. Anything wrong with that?"

"No, but I have mixed feelings about it. If they build a permanent dam, the river would be right up to Daisy's basement. But I like the idea of making a place for people to swim, so long as it's a temporary dam."

"You mean take it down in the winter?"

"Yeah, that's what Mac wanted. He's probably shouting obscenities from his grave right now." I took a sip of coffee, and wondered for the millionth time if Archie had killed Mac over a stupid dam project. How to prove it would be difficult, if not impossible.

Slim and trim in black shirt and slacks, Dustin set a tray down and served our entrées in his usual meticulous style.

"Everything okay?" Dustin asked.

"Oh, don't mind me," I said, "I'm just fired up over a dam project—I mean a…build-a-dam project."

He smiled and hurried back to the kitchen.

After breakfast, David asked what I would like to do for the rest of the day. Suddenly it occurred to me that it was Wednesday, the day of the appreciation barbecue in Ben Lomond. I asked him if he wanted to go and watched his reaction closely. As much as I wanted to go, I didn't want to drag David all the way to Ben Lomond if his heart wasn't in it. But if he wanted to go, that would be wonderful.

David smiled. "Sure, Ben will be there with your Aunt Clara and I guess George will be there, if he can get the time off."

"What does George do?" I asked.

"He's a professor of psychiatry at the university. He has a couple of classes he teaches in the summer session. Forty-two years old and still not married." David shook his head.

"Yeah, he sure knows how to pick 'em. How old is Kit?"

"Not old enough. He needs a 'momma' type." David rolled his eyes.

"He has a mom…." I said.

"Yeah, but not for long. She has stage four cancer. He's not himself these days…won't even go out golfing with the guys."

"I'm surprised he's still helping out at the theater…." I said.

"Yeah, me too," David said, as he helped me into his car. "No golf, no travel, no fun…."

"Maybe Kit's keeping a tight rein on him?"

David shrugged. "I need to pick up a few things at Home Depot before we go up to the valley."

"I have an idea. Can you shop at the hardware store in Ben Lomond? I need to talk to Daisy. You could drop me at her house before you go shopping."

David agreed that was a good plan, and I smiled because I wouldn't have to trot all over Home Depot searching for nuts, bolts and bug spray. And we had plenty of time before the picnic started at two o'clock. I couldn't wait to see Tabatha and Albert. Would they be excited about their new cousin, or would they reject him? I told myself not to worry. It would be okay.

David dropped me off at Daisy's house at one o'clock. The lady of the house came to the door looking miserable, The Girls crushing in behind her. They wagged their tails and sniffed the air until they were sure that Solow wasn't with me.

Daisy walked me to the kitchen where we sat down.

"Well, how did it go?" I asked.

"Unfortunately, Paul has not met his cousins yet…."

"What? I thought…."

"I know, and I was all set to get them together. I went down to Paul's room to invite him upstairs, but he wasn't there." She laid a trembling hand over her mouth.

"So we just wait till he gets back…?"

"In the first place, he's injured," she sniffed. "Second place, he's trying to protect Tabatha. I found a note in his wastebasket." Her voice quivered. "No signature, wouldn't you know!"

"Daisy, don't keep me hanging, tell me what it said."

She pulled a crumpled note out of her pocket and smoothed it with shaky hands.

"It says, 'This is your final warning. Cooperate or I turn you in to animal control—where you belong. The girl is next.' "

I was speechless, as Daisy turned red with anger. She stood, walked to the kitchen sink and began scrubbing a pot vigorously.

"How can people be so cruel?" she sobbed.

"Where's Tabatha?"

"I called Kate and asked her to drive Tab to the theater. I said she pulled a tendon in her leg."

"Nice work, Daisy. We have to protect her."

Daisy slammed the little cooking pot on the counter and grabbed a crusty fry pan. "I can't stand the thought of Pauly out there wandering the mountains in pain. I can't call the police. It's hard enough for him to meet his own cousins, but policemen…forget it!"

"I see what you mean. Can you call him on his phone?"

"No, he didn't take it with him."

The first thing that crossed my mind was that Paul left the phone on purpose because he didn't want anyone to follow him or the pings from his phone.

"Daisy, we need to come up with something we can do for him. Actually, I think I have a plan."

Daisy stopped scrubbing the fry pan. Her eyes widened. "What's your plan, Josephine?"

"Okay, here it is…when David comes back to pick me up in about an hour, I'll invite you to come along with us. At the picnic, you act like you're going to faint and later I'll tell David I'm staying at your house for the night to take care of you. When he leaves, I'll climb the mountain and find Paul."

"The fainting part sounds more like the truth than a lie," she chuckled as she gently set the fry pan on the counter. "Let's get some fresh air." She dried her hands, hooked an arm into mine and we strolled out to the deck. Between the warm sun and the gurgling river, I felt my shoulders relax.

"Daisy, I heard a rumor…."

"Rumors are usually just rumors," she laughed.

"I heard that there was a major scuffle between Frank and Mac a couple of months ago." An awkward silence followed.

Daisy sighed. "It's not a rumor. Frank bought our old Nissan for his daughter. He knew it had over two-hundred-thousand miles on it, but Mac had taken good care of it. Well, the poor girl drove the car into a tree when the brakes failed. Frank wanted his money back plus money for his daughter's injuries."

"Wow, sounds serious," I said.

"She broke her nose on the steering wheel..." Daisy grimaced.

"Ouch!"

"Mac wouldn't give an inch so Frank punched him in the nose—kind of a nose-for-a-nose thing." She rolled her eyes. "Men!"

"Was that the end of it?"

"Not really, since they were both teachers at San Lorenzo Valley High, they were always running into each other."

"What did Frank teach?"

"English," she said, her eyes fixed straight ahead on nothing. "Mac bought a gun. I was against it, but he thought he had to defend us."

David arrived to pick us up, and Daisy seemed happy to be going to a picnic—a nice diversion from her worries about Paul. We arrived at the park at two o'clock to find that most people had been there since one. All the junior actors had been fed hot dogs, hamburgers and strawberry shortcake. Janinne and a couple of associates herded the children back across the street and into the theater, including Tabatha, while the adult volunteers enjoyed ribs, potato salad and homemade apple pie.

Looking around, I noticed Frank, Kate and several other volunteers sitting at the table next to ours—ours being the table Clara and Ben had saved for us. Alicia, Ernie and Trigger arrived, filling our table to capacity.

"Anything wrong, Jo?" Alicia whispered.

"I don't think so...I mean, probably not...."

She didn't look convinced.

Albert crossed the street, walked over to our table and gave us a quick hello. He sat down at Kate's table because they had room for him. We volunteers sat in dappled shade eating food donated by the Ben Lomond Market, barbecued and served up by the local ukulele club. The ribs were extra juicy with sauce that dripped everywhere. My new white eyelet dress was a bull's eye target, even with fifty napkins strategically placed from my chin down to my knees.

As barbecue flames died and the sound of ukuleles-gone-wild woke up the forest, I called it "quits" and excused myself from the table. I grabbed my pursc and Alicia followed me across the street to the theater restrooms. Using one wet paper towel, Alicia wiped a small red speck off her t-shirt while I struggled to clean big sections of my dress using gobs of wet paper towels and commercial-grade pink soap from a dispenser.

"Jo, I think you're making it worse."

"Yeah, you're right." I wiggled out of my dress, dropped it in the sink along with water and more gobs of pink soap. With lots of scrubbing, the material went from red to pink to light pink and took on a janitorial bubblegum smell. The whole dress had turned light pink. I wrung it out with my hands and put it back on.

"Burr!" I looked in the mirror and shivered. "This thing is soaking wet and see-through. I'm going to see if I can dry it somehow. Allie, You go back to the party."

"Okay, Jo." Alicia held her belly laugh until she was outside the building, but I heard it.

Peeking out the restroom door, I watched several groups of children rehearsing their lines and singing songs. Tabatha's song gave me chills, it sounded so pretty—or was it the cold wet dress? I casually walked along the South wall to the open side door and stepped into sawdust. The unoccupied sunny area where props were built was unusually quiet. I sat on a table used for construction, letting the sun warm my pink dress.

Half an hour later, Alicia came to check on me. She said she had smelled janitorial grade barbecue sauce and followed her nose to the little courtyard.

"Very funny! What did you tell David?"

"As little as possible...."

"Good, let's go. I think I'm done."

"You're overdone if you ask me," Alicia laughed.

I darted into the restroom for a quick look at my dress. It was wrinkly but no longer see-through. I raised my chin and crossed the street with Alicia, ready for questioning glances from my friends. Fortunately, Daisy decided to faint as soon as we arrived. I happened to be close enough to catch her before she could slide under the table.

David saw what was happening and took over.

"Daisy, Daisy, are you okay?" he asked her.

Daisy's eyes opened. "What happened?"

"You fainted," David said. "Do you need a doctor?"

"Oh, my goodness. I forgot to take my pills this morning. I'm sorry, but I need to go home right away."

We said quick goodbyes to our friends as Daisy held onto David's arm for support. He walked her to the car and helped her into the back seat. From the front passenger seat, I cranked my head around and looked at Daisy.

She smiled and winked. The great little actors in Ben Lomond had nothing on Daisy.

It was all I could do to not laugh.

With a serious face, I told David I planned to stay and take care of Daisy. He walked her into the house and wished her well.

After a lovely kiss goodbye, I stayed with Daisy and David drove home alone. The first part of my plan had worked. The second part of the plan curled my toes with dread.

Chapter 20

My beautiful Wednesday with David had come to a sudden halt as I watched my love drive away. Our picnic had been cut short because Daisy fainted. Ever thoughtful David had taken care of everything. He drove her home, walked the poor lady to her sofa, fetched her pills from the kitchen and fluffed a pillow for her. Daisy insisted she would be okay if I would stay and help her. David seemed reluctant to leave; but I asked him to take care of Solow for me, and he would never say no to that.

As soon as David drove away, Daisy said, "Josephine, are you going up the mountain wearing that pink dress and those sandals? I would be happy to loan you a pair of my husband's Levis and one of my t-shirts...."

"Throw in a flashlight and a bottle of water and I'll be set to go," I said, with a forced smile. The idea of wearing a dead man's clothes gave me the shivers. Too bad Daisy's legs were a good six inches shorter than mine, but her shirt fit me nicely.

"Daisy, what size shoes do you wear?"

"Six."

"I need an eight and a half...."

"Tab wears an eight and a half," she said, ushering me down the hall to a bedroom taken over by posters of teenage movie stars.

I had my choice of dressy flats, flip flops or tennis shoes. I chose the tennis shoes plus a pair of socks from her dresser drawer.

The front door slammed.

Daisy and I hurried down the hall when we heard Tabatha crabbing to The Girls.

"Why are grown-ups so stupid? It's just a play! I don't want to cut my...oh hello, Josephine, Daisy...." Her eyes went straight to my feet and her tennis shoes.

"You're home early, Tabatha dear. Is everything okay at the theater?" Daisy asked.

Tab looked at the floor.

"I'll talk to the powers that be, tomorrow," I said, "and thanks for letting me borrow your shoes."

Her mouth fell open. "Did something happen to your shoes...?"

I held up my sandals with two-inch heels.

"Not really. I just needed a pair of shoes for hiking."

To Daisy I said, "I'll be right back."

I dropped the sandals on the floor, walked out the front door, angled left around the house and down the path to Paul's door. The lock had not been repaired, and his bedroom was as dark as ever. After feeling my way across the room, I pushed the curtain to one side and fired up the one and only forty-watt light bulb in the room.

The question romping through my head was, did Paul leave because he wanted to go or because he had to? Even Paul could not have healed himself in just two days time. The more I thought about it, the more I could feel his pain. The room was not as neat as usual, so I began straightening things here and there. The wastebasket had not been emptied in a long time and threatened to over flow. I put my foot in the basket and pushed the trash down.

"Oh my G...!" I pulled off Tabatha's tennis shoe. A long string of pink bubble gum connected the shoe to the basket. I grabbed a piece of torn paper from the bin and used it to pull the gum loose from the shoe. I was about to drop the whole wad in the trash when I noticed more crumpled parts to the torn letter. I fished out three pieces and fit them together on the desk, and added the gummy piece, making it an eight by ten rectangle.

The door opened behind me. I jumped and quickly turned around with a stapler in my hand, ready to shoot staples if necessary.

"Josephine, it's me, Tabatha."

It was already too late. She was in the room.

"Hi, Tab, I was just coming out…."

"With a stapler pointed at me?" she grinned.

"Never know who might come into this room."

"Who would want to…it's so gloomy and dark. How come everyone gets so uptight about this room anyway?"

"It's a long story and Daisy is going to tell you about it as soon as she can." That is if I could find Paul before the cougars found him. I quickly grabbed the four-piece letter and stuffed it all in my pocket.

"Let's go upstairs. I want to say goodbye to your Aunt."

"Your truck isn't here…." she said.

"I know. I'm just going for a hike."

Tab looked perplexed, but led me up the path to the house anyway. Daisy stood at the front door and handed me my purse and a backpack. I quickly shoved my purse into the backpack, making it ten pounds heavier.

Daisy told me to watch out for poison oak, and off I went. I walked along the side of the road for a couple of blocks, giving Tab time to lose interest in where I was going. I finally crossed the street, doubled back two blocks, and headed up hill through several private properties bordering fifty miles of dense redwood forest.

At first I powered up the mountain with energy to spare, but ten minutes later my calves cried out for a rest. A saggy log beckoned to me. Ahhh, sitting felt good. I pulled the pieces of paper out of my pocket and laid them out on the log, flattening each one with my hands.

Someone had typed: "I'm giving you five days to make the medicine. Put it in the wood box outside your door Sunday night or the girl will suffer the consequences."

I shuddered at the word, "consequences." Had Mac's death been a consequence? Was this creep referring to Tabatha in the note? It was obvious that someone knew about Paul and his healing ointments and medicines. I remembered David telling me how Mac had bragged about his son in Minnesota. Was there a real son back east or had Mac been talking about Paul?

The only way to find answers to my questions was to find Paul. I charged up the mountain repeating one line over and over, "find Paul, find Paul, find Paul," until my throat was dry and my legs felt like heavy, useless appendages. Another log accommodated my sorry backside, allowing me to catch my breath and guzzle some water.

I figured I had climbed about a mile, which meant I had two more miles to go. It was already five and the sun had disappeared over the western mountains. A flock of gnats swarmed around my face and attacked my eyes. I swatted them away as best I could until I lost my balance and tipped over. The roll down the hill a hundred feet on spongy, leafy mulch would have been fun at age ten, but at age fifty the climb back up was daunting. I blinked and tore my way through the same gang of gnats, barely able to see where I was going.

Suddenly a familiar logging trail appeared, greatly lifting my spirits. I walked the switchbacks for another couple of hours, until another option became available: a wide, level path heading south, where tall palm trees rustled in the fresh evening air. Just having solid flat earth under my feet felt so good.

I felt twenty pounds lighter as I briskly walked the path, opened the gate, marched up the stairs and across a new patchwork of boards on the porch where Paul had fallen through. I knocked on the front door, and a moment later decided he was more likely to be in the back yard. As I rounded the building from the eastern side, I heard the humming of bees and chirping of birds. The place was alive with nature, even after sundown.

"Hey there!" a deep voice rumbled from the shadows.

Even though I was looking for Paul and expected to see him, I jumped at the sound of his voice.

"Paul, how are you?" I looked at his bandaged leg. "Are you healing all right?"

"Oh sure, no problem," he said cheerfully. "How's my mom?"

"Worried. I'm worried too. Who's demanding medicine from you?"

"I wish I knew…," he muttered.

"You're up here making medicine for someone you don't even know?"

"Think about it, Josephine; how many people do I know? I can count them on two fingers," he laughed. "I have to do this. I would never let Tabatha be harmed."

"Yeah, you're right," I said as I sat down on a very rusty cast iron bench. "I just thought you might know who wrote the note."

"I'm afraid that's your department, Josephine. Obviously you found the note—be careful when you figure out who wrote it." He finished placing metal screens over trays of sliced mushrooms and various clumps of greens. He spread a plastic tablecloth over everything to keep the evening moisture out.

“Do you mind if I look at your wound before it’s completely dark out here?”

He sat down next to me and rolled the pant leg up and over his knee. The bandage had leaked blood and needed to be changed. Feeling a bit queasy, I stood up and walked around while Paul ripped tape from his furry leg. He pulled a small jar from his pocket, smeared some brown pasty stuff on the gash and replaced the old bandages with the ones Daisy had put in the backpack.

“Paul, what’s the brown stuff?”

“Honey, a few herbs and essential oils.”

“Daisy sent me up here to bring you back. She really wants you to meet the kids and be one big family.”

Paul hung his head as if invisible weights were pulling it down.

“I think I understand how comfortable you are out here,” I said, “alone, in the middle of all this nature, but Daisy loves you….”

“I know all that, Josephine. I feel plenty of guilt, believe me. But I also feel responsible for Daisy’s health and Tabatha’s safety—that’s why I’m up here making potions.”

“Did you hear that?” I asked. “What’s that rumble?”

“The weather’s changing…might even rain. Help me pack this stuff up, Josephine. I’m taking it inside just in case.”

“You’re kidding! It never rains in the summer…wow, lightning!”

I watched Paul and did what he did, stacking trays and carrying five at a time into the house. He doubled back and grabbed a large paper bag full of just-picked herbs with one hand and a small bucket of honey with the other hand.

"Grab the mud, Josephine." Backlit by lightning, I saw him point to a child-size plastic bucket at the corner of the building.

"I got it!" I grabbed the handle and ran, as sprinkles of rain pelted my face. The only light around came from sporadic flashes of electrical fury skittering across the sky.

After four fast trips by Paul and two slow, stumbly trips by me, everything of value had been hauled into the foyer. Paul lit two fat candles. We spread the trays full of mushrooms and herbs across the length of the check-in counter. Paul placed the bucket of honey in the middle of a platter of water so ants couldn't find it. When everything was covered and safe, he asked what my plan was.

"I think I'll just stretch out on that bench over there," I said.

"I'll be upstairs…lots of work to do," he said as he took the stairs three at a time.

I sat on the bench and pulled my phone out of my purse. Daisy picked up on the second ring.

"Josephine, I'm so glad you called. Is everything okay?"

"Paul is fine. He's very busy making medicine…."

"Thwack!" The floor shook under my feet.

"What's that noise, Josephine?"

"I'm not sure," I said as I walked across the room holding one of the candles in a death grip and the phone to my ear with the other hand. My heavy breathing threatened to put out the flame as I peered out a partly shuttered window. "Wow, lightning must have hit this big tree…and the top part broke off and landed against the hotel. A piece of the tree top is sparking…hang on, Daisy. I'll be right back."

A moment later, I was on the front porch at the far right corner taking a look at the eastern side of the building. There were sparks all right, and the treetop was leaning against the wall. The rain had stopped and fingered clouds parted enough for moonlight to stream down on Paul's vegetable garden.

I dashed into the hotel, picked up the phone and shoved it in my pocket as I charged up the stairs yelling for Paul.

"Hey, Josephine, what's wrong?" We met on the second floor.

"There's a tree up against the building…sparking!" I don't think he understood what I said, but he heard the terror in my voice. I followed him downstairs. He was outside by the time I made it to the foyer. I looked out the window and saw Paul struggling with the treetop. Embers floated in the air, some landed on the grass. He stomped on them with his bare feet.

Leaving the candle behind, I dashed outside to help move the tree. It would have been easier to lift a full-grown horse.

"I'll get water," Paul said as he ran to the back yard. I followed his lead, found a bucket to dunk in the pond and ran back to the flaming treetop. Our bucket brigade lasted about ten minutes before we realized the fire was gaining ground, licking it's way up the eastern wall of the hotel.

"I'll call 911," I said.

Paul kept the buckets of water coming, but even he had to admit it was useless. "Go ahead and call," he choked out the words.

I pulled my phone out and Daisy was still there, waiting for me. "Hello, Daisy, I need you to call 911 for me. Tell them you smell smoke and you see fire up on the mountain."

"I'm outside and I don't see or smell anything…."

"You will if you don't call right away! We're okay and we'll be home soon." I dropped the phone in my pocket.

"Josephine, help me pack up my stuff. I have a backpack and some garbage bags we can fill," Paul shouted. We collected his stuff and packed the bags like a couple of neurotic squirrels just before the first snow.

Paul slipped into his backpack and when my pack was fully loaded, he held it up so I could hook my arms into it. He grabbed two heavy bags full of files, equipment, clothes and little jars and bottles of medicinal ingredients. I quickly jammed more jars of medicine into one bag and picked up another bag full of dried mushrooms and herbs.

Hurrying down the porch stairs, I tried to catch up to Paul. He looked back once. Solow would have been a big help with navigation, but Paul seemed to have superior night vision and a great sense of direction. I left the flashlight in my backpack because Paul had his hand on my elbow, steering me over, under and around the many hazards I couldn't even see. He had made the trip so many times before, I was sure he had it memorized.

Chapter 21

The smell of smoke drifted down the mountain, permeating the air like an unclean intruder. My heart pounded as Paul and I fled his lovely hotel in the middle of the night. A very distant fire siren brought trepidation into the gentle forest. In the grip of my fisted hands were bags of mysterious medicinal ingredients. Paul carried the heavier sacks.

The downward trail, consisting of what seemed like a million cutbacks, finally ended and the slippery down hill slide began. Paul had locked his elbow in mine, allowing me to slip and slide and still stay on course.

"Paul, do you hear something?"

We stopped to listen.

"It's a plane. They're looking for a fire." His sad voice broke my heart.

"Maybe they'll put out the fire quickly...."

"Yeah, and maybe the world won't notice that I'm different."

"Cheer up, we're almost home...your home, that is," I said as the first signs of a pink dawn painted a few smidgens of visible sky. We cut across a couple of properties, crossed the street and hurried down the familiar path to Paul's room where we dropped the bags and slipped out of our backpacks. I slumped into his desk chair feeling like I had just run ten marathons in a row.

Helicopters rumbled in the distance. As soon as one helicopter left, another arrived, and another. Hopefully their buckets of water would hit the old hotel. I was pretty sure the choppers were filling their buckets with water from the local Loch Lomond Reservoir.

"Josephine, thanks for helping me…." Paul's eyes glistened. He looked away. "We have enough supplies here to make a lot of medicine."

"Even for the creep who left the note?"

"I wouldn't deny anyone medicine."

"You're a bigger person than I…."

"That's for sure," he laughed. Then I laughed. Either we were dead tired and a bit rummy, or what I said was really funny. We laughed until our sides hurt, and our eyes puddled with tears.

"Shhh! Did you hear something, Josephine?"

"No…" Just then the door flew open and three people in pajamas stared at us. Daisy was beyond happy to see Paul, but Tabatha and Albert were speechless.

"Tab and Albert, I'd like you to meet my son…."

The kids gazed upward in complete shock, mouths open.

"This is Paul." Daisy made her way across the room to her son and they hugged.

Al looked at me. "Is this for real?"

"Sure is," I said. "Paul is your wonderful cousin…."

"I don't believe it," Al said, turning to walk away.

"Please don't go, Albert dear. I want you two to shake hands and be friends."

Al stayed outside the door but Tab squeezed past him and walked into the room. "I think I've seen you before…in the tree…next to the theater…the night Uncle Mac died," she stuttered.

"Yes, I was there…and I saw you."

"Did you kill our uncle?" Al glared, his young bass voice suddenly jumping up five notches to an embarrassing squeak.

"No, I didn't do it…did you?"

"Of course not…." Al snapped.

"Then we're all on the same side," Paul smiled.

Daisy's eyes jumped from Paul to Albert to Paul and back to Al.

"Al, dear, come here for a minute," she said with more strength in her voice than I had ever heard her use. She motioned with her fingers and smiled gently. Al finally gave in, entered the room and walked the ten steps to her side. She took his hand and pulled it closer to Paul's. Al looked at the giant's hand with fear in his eyes. But the handshake happened, allowing a family connection to finally blossom, with time.

I broke into the magic moment with a touch of reality.

"Someone needs to tune into the local radio station and find out if the fire's coming our way...."

"Oh dear!" Daisy exclaimed, "I'll do that right away...."

"It's okay, Mom," Paul said, sliding into the desk chair with his earphones on. "I'll turn on my radio," he grinned discreetly as he opened up the desktop. "The radio news won't come on for another twenty-five minutes, so we'll use my shortwave radio." Eventually we heard the news through various radio operators who happened to be awake at four-thirty in the morning. It seemed that lightning had touched off several fires in the Boulder Creek and Ben Lomond areas.

Everyone in the room took a breath and waited for details. As we waited, Daisy sat down and the rest of us joined her, sitting should-to-shoulder on the edge of Paul's bed.

An hour later, we heard a staticky voice, "It appears that the last of the fires is out," the voice reported to his buddy. His buddy asked if there were any structures involved. The first guy said he hadn't heard of any. Besides, all the fires happened in very remote areas and had to be put out using helicopters dumping buckets of water.

Daisy, Paul and I sucked in some air and let out a big synchronized sigh. The forest was not on fire and the hotel had not been discovered—but did any of it still exist? I knew Paul would not be happy until he knew for sure what happened to his hotel.

Tab and Al looked mystified—like, what's all the fuss?

Once we had heard that all the fires were out, Paul's cozy room cleared out. Daisy, Al and Tab all went upstairs to their beds, and I curled up on the sofa with The Girls. Being physically exhausted and mentally drained didn't help me to fall asleep. It was early Thursday morning, with three days left before Paul had to put medicine in the wood box for a killer. I was determined not to let the fiend get away with his plan. Did the creep want the medicine so he could analyze it and sell the recipe to Big Pharma for billions, or did he just want to cure an ugly rash?

In my dreams, I saw the killer covered in a lumpy red rash oozing green juice that puddled around his fat ankles. A crow rolled in the juice and instantly became a peacock. An ugly rat marched through the green puddle. Suddenly he became a cuddly panda bear. Out of curiosity, I bent down and touched the green stuff with one finger. The finger turned into a raspberry popsicle.

"Josephine…Josephine…wake up…." Tabatha said as she shook my shoulder.

"Ah…what's wrong, Tab?" I stammered, still half asleep.

"You were making weird noises. Are you all right?"

I looked at my hands. "Yep, I'm okay. Looks like you're going to the theater to practice…."

"It's noon," she said. "I just came home for lunch. Would you like some?"

"You bet I would. Burned a lot of calories on my hike yesterday. Did I dream that Al and Paul shook hands?"

"No, you didn't dream it. It really happened, and I don't care what Al says. I like my new cousin. He's like a gentle giant." She dropped her backpack on a chair and headed for the kitchen. I followed her, hoping for a strong cup of coffee.

"Is Daisy up yet," I asked.

"I doubt it. She needs her sleep," Tabatha said, as she searched the fridge for lunch material. "Coffee pot's over there, Josephine; help yourself."

After a cup of coffee and a tuna sandwich, I settled into a lounge chair on the deck. Tab leaned against the railing near my chair and asked me how well I knew her cousin, Paul.

"I guess there won't be any more secrets around here. I met Paul shortly after I met you. He seems to be honest, intelligent, hard working and very kind. But I don't have to tell you all that because I know you're able to look past his physical appearance and straight into his heart."

"Exactly," she smiled. "I'm proud to have Paul in the family, but why did Aunt Daisy and Uncle Mac adopt him?"

Not wanting to leave anything out, my answer to Tabatha's question took a while to answer. She loved the story of the five-year-old boy finding his way to Daisy's doorstep.

Suddenly Tabatha realized it was getting late. She told me she had to run through a couple of songs with Janinne at two o'clock.

I stood up and told her I would walk with her down to the theater. Tab looked at me like a thirteen-year-old who feels competent to run her own life. But she graciously accepted my offer.

As we tramped through Daisy's neighborhood, Tab and I discussed Albert's reluctance to acknowledge Paul as his cousin. The handshake was a good start, but Al was obviously having a hard time accepting his cousin. Maybe he was intimidated by Paul's unusual height. Maybe Al was used to being the tallest guy around.

Tab explained to me that Al typically needed time to warm up to new people, that he had always been a bit of a loner. By the time we reached town, she and I were like old school chums, talking and giggling about all kinds of things.

"Josephine, is it true that Paul trained The Girls?"

"It's true. They're amazing."

"Uncle Mac told us he trained them."

I kept quiet.

"You probably don't know half the stuff they can do," she said. "If you forget to close a door, one of them will bump it closed. If something happened to Daisy, one of the dogs moves the door latch while the other one pushes the door open. One of them runs for help, the other one stays close to my aunt."

"Amazing!" I said, as we cut across the Ben Lomond Market's parking lot.

"Too bad Uncle Mac didn't take the time to really know Paul…."

"Yeah, his loss," I said.

"We're here… thanks, Josephine…."

"I'm going in too," I said as we entered the theater together. Tab veered left, over to a clutch of friends while I walked straight across the room to Janinne. She sat in a plastic chair, bent over a laptop balanced on her lap. She looked up.

"Josephine, are you here to paint?"

"No, I wanted to talk to you about Tabatha's...."

"I bet I can guess, you're worried that her hair will be cut short? Well, that's been taken care of. I just finished rewriting her part," Janinne smiled. "She will play the part of Penny Pamilton. What do you think?"

"That's brilliant...and she won't have to cut her hair," I said.

"Now I have to get the new title to the printer before they go into production. I'm changing the name of the play from Peter Pamilton to Penny Pamilton." Janinne leaned over her laptop and hit the keys at a furious rate.

Out of curiosity and habit, I made my way past groups of child actors and stage equipment, all the way to the back room. My head automatically tilted upward, glancing at the attic door. The door stood wide open like a hungry lion's mouth waiting for Thumper to hop over the threshold. I climbed the stairs, stood on the landing and slammed the door shut.

"Hey, what-cha doin?" a voice yelled.

I quickly opened the door and apologized to the little fella. As I thumped down the stairs, Al strolled into the room. He came up to me and apologized for the way he had acted with Paul.

"I think Paul understands," I said. "He's not into quick superficial friendships either. Both of you are deeper than that."

"Thanks, Josephine. Daisy sent me down here to see if you want me to drive you home."

"That would be wonderful, Albert. I was wondering if I would have to hitchhike or take the Greyhound." We both laughed.

Chapter 22

Early Friday morning I woke up realizing there were only two more days until Paul would meet up with the person who threatened to hurt Tabatha if he didn't get his meds. There was no way I wouldn't be there to see who it was and call the police. But until then, I had a few more props to paint. I figured we would finish the job in the next three or four days.

The house phone rang.

I sprang out of bed at the speed of a fifty-year-old woman still a bit foggy from bouncing in and out of a good night's sleep. Standing barefoot on the cold kitchen linoleum, I picked up the phone.

"Ah, Josephine…?"

"Yes, who's this?" I didn't really need to ask since there was no way I wouldn't recognize the Texas drawl.

"Remember me…Kit Malone? I'm George's fiancée…."

"Of course I remember you. How are you, Kit?"

"Well, at first I wasn't gonna call you, but what the heck. I need advice from an older person…not that you're so old or anythang…."

"That's okay, Kit, I can take it. We have about twenty-five years between us. George is an older person…you can't talk to him?"

"That's what this is about. He's actin' more strange everyday."

"Kit, would you like to meet and have lunch with me today?"

"That would be great," her voice cracked, and I heard a sniffle.

"See you at the Ben Lomond Park at one o'clock."

"Thanks, I need to ask you somethin'." She hung up.

I dropped the phone into its cradle, and let Solow out for his first Fluffy chase for the day. I smiled, remembering my extended and hard-earned bubbly bath the night before. It had worked miracles for sore leg muscles, tension and all-around filth.

Still in my pajamas, I tossed Daisy's shirt, Mac's pants and Tab's tennies and socks into the washing machine.

Most mornings, a hot shower and cup of coffee would set me on the path of accomplishment for the day. But this time there was a problem—no hot water. "Dang!" I muttered to myself, as I trudged down the hall to my room, threw on a set of paint clothes, slipped into a pair of sandals and headed for the kitchen.

Mr. Coffee gurgled its plop, plop song as I scrounged for breakfast food in the fridge. When I finally had a nice hot breakfast prepared, Solow barked to come back in the house. Because I was in the habit of sharing a bite or two with him at every meal, we feasted on bacon and eggs together.

I tossed the load of laundry into the dryer, sipped my coffee and read the front page of the newspaper while Solow digested his little bites of breakfast under the table.

There was a quick knock on the back door just before it opened and David walked in.

I stood up and we hugged.

"How's Daisy doing?" he asked.

"Oh, Daisy…she's okay…I decided to stay the night with her just to make sure."

"How did you get home yesterday…?" he asked.

"Albert drove me home in Daisy's little Fiat. He's a very good driver, for a sixteen-year-old."

"Am I going to see you tonight?" he asked.

"Oh no, look at the time! Sorry, Sweetie, it's eight and I have to go to work. I'll be staying with Aunt Clara and Ben until Monday. And the good news is, we'll have finished our work at the theater before I see you Monday night."

We held onto each other and kissed. David handed me my backpack and purse, and walked me outside carrying a garbage sack containing Solow's bed and bowl and a smaller sack of borrowed clothes. Like the good neighbor and good man that he was, he loaded everything into the truck bed and pulled the snug top down.

Solow ran to the passenger door, and I hoisted him into his seat.

When I was settled into my seat, I remembered something and rolled the window down. "Oh, David, I forgot to tell you. Something's wrong with my hot water—there isn't any."

He rolled his eyes and told me to stay out of trouble.

"Trouble? What kinda trouble is he talkin about?" I said to Solow, laughing and singing to old songs on the radio as we bumped along country roads and then Highway One with its normal congestion. Highway Nine, one of the curviest roads in the universe, was slow and go all the way to Ben Lomond.

I braked the truck behind Alicia's Volvo. We hurried across the street and into the theater. Alicia turned her head, looked down on us from her ladder and said, "Hi, Jo, get stuck in traffic?"

"Yep. Who's the new guy out there with George?"

"Frank's dad. Frank had to quit because his malaria is acting up. Kate said he got it on a trip to Brazil about ten years ago."

"Does his dad know carpentry?" I wondered out loud as Kate walked up behind me.

"Lucky worked as a carpenter most of his life, and he volunteered to take his son's place," Kate said.

"Bah…loooo," Gypsy added.

"Poor Frank," Alicia said.

"But 'lucky' for the theater to get a replacement so quickly, no pun intended," I said, as I climbed up a ladder next to Alicia's. We could easily have been mistaken for a high-flying clown act. Dropping my brush full of paint was bad enough, but as I retrieved it and re-climbed the ladder, I remembered that Solow needed his water dish so I headed back down, forgetting the last rung. I thunked to the floor, still standing but off balance. My shoulder hit Alicia's ladder, causing her little pot of red paint to throw itself against the floor and roll, leaving a trail for the three little wild monsters to run through.

I don't remember screaming, but suddenly Kate and Lucky were there to catch Alicia if they had to. Lucky grabbed me by the elbow and held on till I stopped swaying.

"Thanks, Lucky," I giggled. "All I had with breakfast was coffee."

"Coulda fooled me," he laughed, as his belly quivered under a Smokey the Bear t-shirt. "What's your name little girl?"

"Goldie Locks, but you can call me Josephine."

Lucky grinned, exposing a perfect set of plastic teeth.

"And this is my friend, Alicia…."

"Pleased to meet ya, miss," he bowed and whipped off an imaginary hat. Too bad he was too old to be an actor in the play. From the twinkle in his eyes down to his red shoelaces, he was a character. Funny how a fun guy like Lucky could have such a quiet son like Frank.

I heard a commotion at the entrance door and turned to see Daisy walk in with The Girls behind her.

"I'll be right back, Allie," I said, and met up with Daisy in the center of the room. Daisy looked winded so we walked over to a couple of plastic chairs pushed up to the North wall and sat down.

Solow joined The Girls as they sat close to Daisy.

"Josephine, you're looking pink cheeked today."

"I just had a run-in with a ladder, but everything's okay now. How's Paul…?"

"Well, you know Paul," Daisy sighed. "He left sometime during the night. I'm sure he's checking to see if the hotel is still there. I'm glad he finally met his cousins, but I can see that it won't change him. Even if the hotel is gone, he'll always be a mountain man and a loner."

"And he'll always keep in touch with you, Daisy, because you'll always be his mom and he'll always be your little boy at heart. I have to get back to work now. Anything I can get for you before I go?"

"No, dear, I just wanted to thank you for bringing Paul home. And…I want to watch you paint."

I no sooner made it up the ladder than Aunt Clara arrived with Sara. The shiny black Rottie wore her colorful "everyday's a party" scarf around her thick neck. Clara left Sara with the pack of canines snoozing under a table and walked over to the stage area to greet us. I threw her a kiss from the fifth rung and she sent one back.

Three little hooligans pulled Clara by her shirttail over to a table where bows, arrows and hatchets had been constructed out of paper maché. Too bad Daisy didn't have the energy that Clara had. But the next time I looked, Daisy was helping the boys paint their bows and arrows, as all four dogs and Gypsy rested under the worktable.

The Ben Lomond firehouse siren blasted as usual at noon; and one hour later, we took a lunch break in the park. Clara and Janinne had their hands full with two picnic tables of children, plus three overactive little boys whooping it up until their mothers finally arrived to take them home.

Our table was much quieter—just the occasional hysterical outbursts of laughter brought on by Lucky's jokes and pranks. I had never heard Daisy's high-pitched laughter before. Even somber Professor George Hathaway belly laughed several times.

Lunchtime resembled a party until I suddenly remembered my lunch date with Kit. I looked toward the street and there she was, sitting in the Camaro watching us. My legs slowly unscrambled, allowing me to climb out from the table. Alicia scooted over, giving me room to swing my body around, slide off the bench and hoof it across the street.

Just as I came up to the car, Kit revved the powerful Camaro engine and started to pull out from the curb.

"Kit, wait a minute," I yelled as I slapped the side of the car with my hand.

The Camaro jerked to a stop. Kit rolled her window down.

"Get in, I know a good place to eat."

I climbed into the passenger seat, the woman hit the gas and the back of my head whacked the headrest. Luckily it was impossible to speed through Ben Lomond because of crosswalks, traffic, speed limits and cops. We only made it two blocks before red and blue lights began following us.

"Now what rock was that opossum hiding under?" Kit growled, as she pulled to a stop at the curb just two blocks away from the theater.

A deputy sheriff walked up to her open window.

"License, ma'am…."

"Hello Lieutenant," she cooed, looking innocently unruffled.

"I'm not a lieutenant. License please."

"Well you look like a lieutenant," she said, batting her eyes at Sergeant Smothers.

I cringed in my seat as the bull-stuff got deeper.

"Hand me my purse, would ya, darlin'?" she said to me.

I handed over the purse and she proceeded to dig through it, pulling out bottles of nail polish, lipsticks, blue mascara and a fifty-dollar bill which she held out to Smothers.

"Is this yours?" she asked as if he had accidentally dropped the money in her lap.

"It's not mine," he said in a convincingly stern voice.

"Okay, here's my license, now throw the book at me," she whimpered.

I was about to gag.

The sergeant leaned down and looked across Kit, at me. "Ms. Stuart, anything new in the Mackie case?"

"Nothing yet," I smiled, knowing that I would find out who murdered Mac very soon. All I had to do was catch the murderer picking up Paul's medicine. I pictured myself hiding in the dark behind a large rhododendron bush, waiting for the perp to show up at the wood box.

"Maybe the three little boys who locked the girl in the attic also murdered Mac," Smothers suggested, his lips curling into a wry smile.

Kit finally found her driver's license and paperwork and handed everything to the smirking sergeant. He took it to his cruiser and radioed the mother ship to see if she was an axe murderer or had any other bad habits.

By the time the officer returned, the interior of the Camaro had heated up and we were sweating profusely.

As soon as Kit got off with a warning, she fired up the AC and drove six miles north to a little taco place in Boulder Creek. The owner of the hole-in-the-wall restaurant had a big Texas smile and heavy accent. As far as I could see he was the greeter, cook and server all rolled into one heavy-set fifty-year-old.

"You probably already guessed this is my dad, right?"

"No, but I guessed he's from Texas…."

"He retired from the Air Force and needed something to do," Kit said stiffly, as we sat down at a little table for two outside on the patio.

She ordered a coke and chips with hot salsa.

I ordered iced tea.

Kit spread her long-fingered hands on the cool glass tabletop.

"You're not wearing your ring today," I said.

"That's what I wanted to talk to you about. George asked me to give the stupid ring back. Said he couldn't think about gettin' married now with his momma so sick and all. He's a real mama's boy."

"What did you want to ask me, Kit?"

"Have you been messin' round with my fiancé?" Her eyes had become tearful slits as she clenched her jaw.

"What are you talking about…?" I stammered.

"Frank told me you like to flirt with all the guys."

"That's crazy, Kit. He must have had a fever when he said that. You know he has malaria…."

'No, I didn't know." She sat in silence for a moment. "Do you really think Frank was out of his mind when he said that? I remember it was a really hot day, and he was sweating all over his shirt…I didn't know he was sick."

"It's going to be okay, Kit. Give George some space. He'll miss you and be back, you'll see." It struck me funny how easily I handed out advice when I was so conflicted about my own situation with David. He was every woman's dream, so why did I spend so much time away from him? Would I ever mature to the point that I could ignore solving a murder mystery and just stay home with my man?

Chapter 23

My jitters Saturday morning were like Friday morning's jitters, only stronger. Feelings of fear, excitement and nervousness gripped me because there was only one more day till Sunday, the day that the murderer would come calling and be caught. I imagined capturing the perp for the hundredth time, wondering if I should bring the Sheriff in on it in case there was some rough stuff. If Paul stayed with me on the stakeout, and if he could be tough, maybe I wouldn't need the cops. But I didn't know if Paul had a tough side. My head buzzed with questions, leaving me to follow my instincts.

Finally, I put aside my worries, let Solow and Sara out the back door and found a post-it note from Clara stuck to the toaster. She said Ben was taking her out for breakfast and she would see me at the theater at nine.

Thankfully, Aunt Clara's bathroom shower was new and quite luxurious as opposed to my very old and tired shower-bathtub setup at home, the one with no hot water. Thinking about hot water reminded me that I needed to call David. I would have called him Friday night, but Clara and Ben took me to an outdoor concert in Felton. We didn't get home until midnight.

I towel dried my hair, wrapped the towel around my body and trotted down the hall to the guest room. I dug through my backpack for clean clothes, and dressed myself in shorts and a t-shirt smeared with at least five colors of paint across the front. My shirts did the normal cover-the-body-thing but were also used for wiping my painty hands while standing on a ladder eight or ten feet above the floor. Alicia, on the other hand, never had a spot on her shirt—or her hands.

My cell phone rang.

Quickly, I rummaged through my purse, found the phone and smiled when I heard David's voice on the line.

"Hi, David, we saw the best concert last night…."

"I thought you didn't like concerts," he quipped.

"Aunt Clara talked me into going and the music was terrific and I saw lots of people I know, like Janinne and her family and Kyle and his girlfriend and…."

"Josie, I have to go in a minute. I just wanted you to know that I installed a new water heater and now you have plenty of hot water."

"Thank you, David. I can't wait to finish this job so that we can have more time together."

"Call me tonight," he said and hung up, but that was okay because I was in a hurry too.

Leaving Solow behind with his lovely Sara, I drove to Ben Lomond and checked in at the theater just a wee bit after nine. Alicia and Kyle were already on their ladders painting faux bricks. My job was to add highlights and shadows to their wall of sponged-bricks. One brick at a time, I painted a lighter shade of dirty red across the top and down the right side. A much darker dirty-red line went down the left side and across the bottom of each brick.

Aunt Clara walked up to the wall and touched one of the bricks to see if it had volume.

"Looks like our bricks are a success," Alicia laughed.

"Just checking," Clara giggled. "Getting warm in here, don't you think?" Ben had brought Clara's sewing machine to the theater and set it up on one of the worktables. She gulped some water from a bottle and went back to sewing costumes. The hum of her machine was drowned out periodically by sawing and hammering outside.

George and Lucky were building a ten-foot by twelve-foot stage, five-feet tall with multiple layers of steps leading up to it. This was the "Hamilton" part of the Peter Pan story, which became the Penny Pamilton story.

We took a lunch break between brick making and step painting.

All the volunteers headed next door to the Ben Lomond Market to buy sandwiches and cold drinks. Kate brought her own lunch and saved a picnic table for the "volunteers," as the park was well-used on weekends by the town's people.

As usual, all the young actors had the weekend off, giving the volunteers more room to concentrate on the remaining work. Sitting at our tree-shaded table, Kate filled us in on what still needed to be painted and gave us more photos and sketches to help with the process. She ate her lunch, explained the work, entertained Gypsy and didn't slop any mustard or secret sauce on her shirt.

"Jo, looks like you added another color to your t-shirt," Alicia said. "Kind of a mustard shade of yellow…."

Kyle snickered.

"That's the beauty of wearing a paint shirt, every smear looks like paint even if it's catsup or mustard," I said, leaning forward and taking another bite of my drippy pastrami sandwich. "Hey, isn't that Archie going into the theater?"

Alicia and Kyle turned their heads and shrugged their shoulders.

"I wonder what he's doing…." I said to no one in particular.

"Archie's involved in the other theater groups that use the building ten months out of the year," Kate explained. "Sometimes he just shows up and looks around to make sure we haven't abused the fine furniture."

"Like the plastic chairs and fifty-year-old tables?" Alicia asked.

"Yeah, but I think he just likes the energy created by actors and musicians—even the volunteer work crew," she laughed.

"Sounds like he needs a job," Alicia said.

"Actually," Kate took a gulp of iced tea, "Archie is one of those high energy people. He sells cars for a living, but he does a lot of volunteer work at his church and Food for the Hungry in Felton, plus he's on the School Board, the Water Board and caretaker of the Ben Lomond Theater."

Her description of Archie did not match the one in my head. Archie was obviously a better man than I had given him credit for.

Eventually my painters and I left the woodsy river park for an afternoon of work in the theater. I spotted Archie through the side door schmoozing with the carpenters. He held a large piece of wood while Lucky ran his saw through it. We couldn't hear their conversations, but the exploding laughter could be heard over all other noises.

Archie finally left the building, but on his way out, he smiled at me and said, "Hello," to Daisy and The Girls as they squeezed past him. The Girls looked around for Solow and Sara, while Daisy watched me brush rusty brown paint on the almost life-size pirate ship. The upper part had already been painted on the wall and the bottom half of the ship, made out of plywood, concealed various platforms for young singers. It was up to us to make the whole thing look like an old sailing ship.

Just ten minutes into their visit, The Girls had their tongues out, panting like crazy. Daisy followed me to the sink in the back room where I filled a bucket with water and set it down for The Girls. Wanda, wearing a forest green collar, went first. It seemed to me she was the alpha dog.

As usual, Daisy needed to sit for a while to catch her breath. We sat on the bench at the bottom of the stairs leading to the attic. I asked her if she had ever been up there.

"Oh my no, but I might someday. I'm getting stronger everyday," she smiled. "My oncologist says there are no traces of cancer. He can't figure it out," she laughed.

"What about the seizures…and diabetes…?"

"I haven't had a seizure in over a year and my diabetes is under control as long as I take the medicine Paul makes for me…and watch my diet, of course."

Wanda growled under her breath as Willow tried to drink from the bowl. Ms. Alpha slowly lapped up more water and Willow whined.

"Willow, go!" Daisy said waving her arm once to the left.

Willow turned, trotted up the stairs, and laid her body down on the wooden landing in front of a paint-deprived partially open attic door and let out a dramatic sigh.

"Daisy, that's the first time I've seen The Girls act like normal dogs."

"I try to practice Paul's rules and keep them in line. But today, I think Willow was just too hot to behave. Willow, come," she said with a flick of her wrist. Willow lumbered down the steep steps and lapped up water while Wanda ran up the stairs and sniffed around the door.

I stood up. "Daisy, I have to get back to work."

"Maybe I'll see you later at the house?" she said.

"Maybe…" Out of habit, I looked up to the top of the stairs. "Ah, where's Wanda?"

"Oh my, she probably picked up Tabatha's scent in the attic, or Mac's. Wanda, come!"

Wanda poked her head out the door, and bolted down the steps to sit next to Willow, like two beautiful bookends without the books. Daisy and The Girls left the backroom while I gathered paint for the next part of the pirate ship. Again, out of habit, I looked up to the attic.

"Well, how did that happen?" I asked myself as I trudged up to the landing and pulled the door wide open.

"Jo, still snooping around?" Kyle stood by the sink with a silly grin on his face.

"Not really," I said, making my way down the stairs. "Have you mixed up a darker shade of brown for the ship? The paints we need are over there by the sink. And don't forget to mix up an 'old gold' for the hardware."

"No problem, Jo," Kyle said, as he began opening odd cans of paint, and pouring random amounts of color into a half-gallon container. Knowing Kyle, we would create the perfect brown for our project. It went without saying that he would also mix up a lighter version of the brown for highlighting. We would use black to establish the size and length of the faux boards. Because of the hot weather the acrylic paint would be dry within a minute or two of being applied, making the blending process difficult.

"Looking good, Josephine," Kate said, passing by.

"Bah…looo," Gypsy laughed and blew kisses as she rode on Kate's back out the front door.

I looked around. Unless the carpenters came up with another structure, we painters were almost finished. Just one big ship to paint; two days work at the most.

The place was stone quiet because Clara and I were the last to leave. Clara asked if I would stop by Daisy's house on our way home. She needed to talk to Tabatha about costume changes brought about by a sudden gender switch of the main character.

"Josephine, what kind of hair style would a Penny Pamilton have?"

"Braids, of course…and bangs." I could see it clearly.

Aunt Clara stared at the ceiling of my truck for a moment. Finally, she said, "Yes, I can see that. Tomboyish, but still pretty."

We arrived at Daisy's house just before a familiar-looking Camaro pulled to a stop behind us. Tab hopped out and the red car thundered away. Tabatha greeted me and took the bag of borrowed clothing I finally remembered to give back to her.

"Tab, how do you know Kit?"

"She's my friend Hanna's big sister…by twelve years. I was invited to a sleepover with Hanna and some of her friends. Kit took us to the boardwalk today. It was so much fun…."

"You look like you're ready for a nap."

"Yeah, we didn't get much sleep last night," she laughed, and ran into the house to tell Daisy all about it.

Clara climbed out of the passenger seat, and we followed Tab all the way through the house to the deck where The Girls greeted us briefly and then returned to Daisy's side. Daisy stood up and gave Aunt Clara a warm hug. A moment later, Clara gasped, sounding like she was choking as she sucked in some air and plopped down on a bench.

"What's the matter, Auntie?" I asked, looking around to see what had stunned her. In a shady corner of the deck, Paul sat on a chaise lounge with his knees up to his chin. He smiled cautiously.

Daisy walked over to Paul and laid a hand on his shoulder, as if to keep him from running away.

"Clara, I'd like you to meet my son, Paul."

Aunt Clara practically leaped across the deck to Paul for a hug. As he stood up and straightened, taller and taller, her jaw dropped. But Clara's upward gaze of astonishment instantly became the sweet motherly smile and composure I knew so well.

"Paul, how is your leg wound?" I asked

"Completely healed," he smiled.

I turned to Aunt Clara. "Paul is a healer. He makes all kinds of medicines."

Clara's eyes brightened. "Do you do bunions, my dear?"

"Maybe someday," he replied with a serious expression, except for the twinkle in his eye.

Daisy, Tab and Clara went to the kitchen to find something cold to drink and to discuss Tabatha's costume, giving me a chance to talk to Paul alone. He said he had finished making the medicine and planned to leave it in the wood box Sunday night.

"How did you know what type of medicine to make?" I asked.

"I got a note a couple of weeks ago asking for medicine to treat lung cancer. I ignored it. But the next note—the one you found—I couldn't ignore."

"How do you know you can cure this person?"

"I don't know for sure, but I cured Daisy of lung cancer. Mac used to be a heavy smoker, and my poor mom got the disease."

"Paul, did you know that Mac bragged about his son to his friends?"

"Yeah, his son living in Minnesota," he laughed. "Maybe the guy I'm dealing with figured Mac's son would come home for his dad's funeral. But how did he know about the basement? The note had been shoved under my door."

"Have you been followed by anyone?"

"Nope," he scratched his head. "At least, I don't think so."

"Paul, I've been dying to know if the hotel is still there…."

"Not much of it. I think the basement might be okay once the burnt timbers are removed. Redwood is funny, some of the big beams didn't even burn. To your question, some of the hotel still exists but it's not much good."

"So what are you going to do now?" I asked, feeling heartbroken for Paul's loss.

"Actually, it's not so bad," he smiled, "the fire didn't even touch the potting shed that sits a couple of hundred feet behind the hotel. The shed was built like the hotel, big and sturdy. It's about twenty-five feet long and fifteen feet wide. I had already started cleaning it up and making repairs before the fire happened."

"That's great news, Paul. Will you go back to growing herbs and such?"

"Couldn't stop if I tried," he laughed. "I have a lot more I want to learn and do. When I'm in the forest, I'm more in touch with my instincts and intuition."

Half an hour later, Aunt Clara walked up to me saying that all the costume issues had been resolved and suggested we stop at the take-out barbecue place in Boulder Creek on our way home.

Chapter 24

"Did you say the young man is only seventeen?" Clara asked as we sped north through the San Lorenzo Valley on our way to Boulder Creek to pick up a delicious barbecued dinner.

"Yep, Paul is seventeen and smarter than you can imagine," I said, as my truck careened around turn after turn for the next ten minutes. We entered the historic lumber town of Boulder Creek and pulled to a stop in front of the BBQ Pit, a small restaurant located halfway down Central Avenue.

Clara climbed down from her seat.

I rounded the truck and asked her what kind of barbecued food she had in mind.

"Ben loves the ribs. He could eat them every night of the week," she chuckled. "But I'll call him and make sure that's what he wants."

I handed Aunt Clara my phone. She didn't own a cell phone because she wanted to express her personal repudiation of the worldwide phone craze.

"The stupid phone won't ring…." she complained.

I looked at it. "No wonder, no bars. Remind me to charge it when we get to the house."

She rolled her eyes in disgust. "Oh well, I'm sure he will enjoy the ribs. What are you having, Josephine?"

"Ribs, of course."

Once we were inside the restaurant reading the menu written across a four by five-foot blackboard, I realized there were many types and flavors of ribs I had never heard of. I decided to go with the basic House Ribs with a tossed green salad and sweet potato fries. Clara followed my example and ordered two more rounds of the same.

I carried a cardboard box filled with containers of ribs and fries, and Clara carried a large plastic container full of salad. I held the salad while she climbed into her seat, handed her the box of hot food and then the salad. She placed the box over her feet and put the container of salad on her lap.

"Oh my, this box is hot on my feet."

"Don't worry, we'll be home soon." I put the truck in 'Drive,' turned on the headlights and rolled through town. Four blocks later, we turned left onto Big Basin Highway. We had covered about five miles of windy road when I checked the time on the dash. It was eight o'clock and darker than a tar pit.

Suddenly the headlights glommed onto a deer leaping into the road. Disoriented, the animal barely missed the right front fender of the truck as I jerked the wheel to the left, stomped on the brakes and yanked the wheel back sharply to the right. It all happened in two-seconds time. In the third second, my truck slid down a bank, rolled over once and slid sideways in slow motion until a tree trunk stopped our descent.

Aunt Clara was still screaming when we came to an abrupt stop. Reaching in her direction to try to comfort her, I felt something warm and wet. Was she bleeding? Was I?

"Auntie, are you all right?"

"Yes, I think so," she said in a quivery voice. "How are you, dear?"

"Don't say the word, 'deer' around me after what that stupid deer did to us," I cried, shutting the engine down and popping my seatbelt loose.

"I can't see a thing, Josephine. Am I blind, or are your lights not working?"

"I think the lights aren't working—or else we're both blind."

I tried to pat Clara on the shoulder, but again I felt the warm sticky liquid. "Are you sure you're not bleeding?"

"I'm a bit shaken, but I don't think I'm bleeding anywhere."

Leaning against the steering wheel, I ran my right hand along the dashboard until I felt the glove compartment. It popped open easily. I felt around for the flashlight.

"Josephine, thank goodness for some light."

"Oh my God! Auntie you're covered in barbecue sauce."

She licked a finger. "So I am…delicious. At one point, I remember pulling the box off my head," she laughed. Only my aunt could laugh after such a scary ride down a fifty-foot embankment.

I pointed the flashlight around the cab and then out the windows to see what our situation was. It wasn't pretty. Clara's window was smack up against the trunk of a giant redwood. Actually it was the kindly tree that had stopped us twenty feet short of rolling into the river.

Since homes along the Big Basin Highway were few and most of the area was undeveloped forest, we saw no lights at all.

I tried my door. It opened but not without a lot of effort. I let it close, and waited several minutes for my limp shaky legs to get a grip. Reminding myself that we were not injured helped me to strengthen my resolve to get Aunt Clara home. After all, she was seventy-five-years old. How much wilderness could she take?

"Where are you going, Josephine?"

"Just looking around. If this bank had been any steeper, we wouldn't be eating ribs in my truck tonight, we would be swimming upstream with the trout." I groaned against the weight of the door as I squeezed my Reubenesque middle-aged body out of the truck.

My sandals sunk a couple of inches into plowed earth. Something tickled my ankle. I brushed it away. Another tickle. I pointed the light on my filthy feet as little ants investigated my ankles. I brushed them off as best I could.

Deciding to put off climbing up to the highway until later, I pulled the cab door open a few inches and little-by-little inserted parts of my body, beginning with shoulders, into the truck. With the driver's side resting higher than Clara's side, gravity had the upper hand and holding the door open was a Herculean task. Once I was finally settled inside, I pointed the light at Clara. Seeing my aunt covered in sauce, I didn't know whether to laugh or cry.

"I'm starving," she said, announcing that she was going to start with salad and go to the ribs and fries later. Obviously we would not be delivering dinner to Ben that night, so why not enjoy a good dinner before it went cold? I understood Clara's logic because I actually had more in common with her than with my own mother.

We munched on salad, ribs and fries without worrying about spillage. There was so much mess already, what would it matter?

"So what did you think of Paul?" I asked.

"Oh my, he's a big boy," she laughed, wiping sauce off her forehead with a paper napkin.

I leaned over and wiped a big red blob off the left side of Aunt Clara's face.

"Thank you, dear…sorry, I used the 'deer' word," she laughed. Only my auntie could have fun with an unfortunate situation like the one we were in. "Paul is a gentle soul, don't you think?"

"I think you're very perceptive." But I wondered if that gentle soul was too gentle. Would he help me capture a murderer? We ate like lumber jacks and still had plenty of food left over for breakfast.

"Smack, swish."

I watched Clara flick a couple of ants off of her arm. Moments later, it was an all out fight, hundreds of little ants against the big Aunt. I helped her fight off the insects wherever I could. The fight raged as more ants got the memo about a lady covered in sweet barbecue sauce. Clara squealed, swatted and swore, but the ants kept coming, occasionally crossing over the console to my side.

"Get me out of here," Clara moaned.

"Yeah, we gotta get out…." I pushed my door open with one leg, stuck my rear out the door, stretched and pushed until I was standing on soft dirt, the door leaning hard against my back. "Auntie, give me your hand. I'm going to pull you over the console."

"And I'm going to fly home," she laughed, giving me her hand. Inch-by-inch she maneuvered her body up and over the center cup holder obstruction. Her back was flush with the ceiling, her legs still tangled up with a box of leftovers on the passenger side. Finally, Clara plunged forward, face first, into the driver's seat. Her legs went up behind her as I tugged on both arms with all my strength.

"Don't stop now, Josephine, I'm stuck," she shrieked.

Noticing that her muumuu was caught on the gearshift, I bellowed out my instructions. "Auntie, take a deep breath, unhook your muumuu…now bring your knees up and push your feet against the passenger door. I'll pull from this end."

"The ants are getting me…hurry!" she cried.

"Almost there. Now keep going, let your body slide out the door and down to the ground…I'll catch you."

"But that's where the ants came from…."

"The minute you get your legs out of the truck, we get up and run down to the river. Ants don't swim."

"Run? Do you know how old I am?"

"Yes, I do, three years younger than Mom. This little sprint will qualify you for the Guinness Book of World Records—oldest woman to be chased by ants into a river." By that time we were laughing hysterically.

The moment Clara's flip flops hit the dirt, I helped her to stand up straight. We rounded the truck and half slid, half tumbled a few yards down the sandy bank to a body of slow moving black water. Clara quickly pulled her muumuu up over her head and tossed it aside. I took off my shorts, t-shirt and sandals while swatting ants. Clara shook off her flip flops and rushed into the cold water. But a couple of feet of water wasn't good enough for my poor aunt, who had sauce and ants stuck to her head and all the way down to her toes.

Clara sat down in the water, and splashed it against her neck. In desperation, she finally leaned forward and dunked her head several times, working the water through her thick hair with her fingers.

My feet mucked around in the river bottom, stepping on all kinds of imagined critters. But the ants were real, so I splashed water on my belly and dipped my hind end into the river. When I stopped feeling the ants, I climbed out of the water and picked up the flashlight. The light went wonky as I shivered and shook.

"Good news, Aunt Clara; your hair is now pink instead of red."

Clara shivered and staggered up to dry sand.

"Stay here, Auntie, I'll look for something to dry you off. Sorry, I need to take the light with me," I said, as I charged up the bank to my truck, pushed up the bed cover and grabbed a large canvas tarp speckled with dry paint. I tucked the roll of canvas under one arm, picked up a plastic bag full of paint rags and hurried back to Aunt Clara. She was still sitting on a rock where I left her.

In a stuttery, shivery voice Clara said, "What are we doing out here, half naked in the forest?"

"It's okay, Auntie, just think of your underwear as a stylish bikini. And look, the moon is coming up." I pointed to a full silver moon traveling across a little piece of sky surrounded on all sides by a canopy of treetops.

Just looking at the moon boosted our spirits—never mind that we could finally see without using the flashlight.

I dried Clara's hair with the rags while she dried her body with more rags. We took our discarded pieces of clothing down to the water, swished them around until the sauce and the ants were gone and hung them on tree branches to dry.

We curled up on half of the tarp and pulled the rest of it over us. "Warm as a bug in a rug," Clara giggled.

"Home is where the heart is," I chimed in, grateful to be alive.

Chapter 25

It was not my usual Sunday morning, waking up to bright sunshine filtering through leafy branches, the sound of water flowing nearby and my Aunt Clara snoring like hogs in a holler. I blinked several times, not able to comprehend what I was seeing. A long shadow fell across the tarp Clara and I were wrapped up in, like mummies in a blanket.

I started to pull back the canvas, but stopped when I saw my clothes hanging on a tree branch a few yards away.

The shadow moved away, then returned.

Looking up toward the early morning sunrise, I saw Paul handing my clothes to me. He said, "Good morning, Josephine."

"Thank you, Paul. How did you know where we were?"

"Ben called Daisy and she called me because nobody knew what had happened to you two. Your aunt snores pretty loud," he chuckled. "We all knew you two were headed up Highway Nine and then Big Basin Highway to Ben's place, so I walked all night and found evidence of a vehicle going over the side of the road. Broken tree branches, tire tracks and something in the air that smelled like barbecue."

As Paul explained how he found us, I glanced at Clara's hair in the morning light. "Oh my…look at that pink hair!" I giggled.

Clara moved, the snoring stopped and she opened her eyes.

"Am I dreaming…or is that Paul standing over us?"

"Actually, it's a dream come true. He found us, he actually found us!" I shouted. "Paul, why don't you check on the truck while Clara and I put our clothes on?"

Paul left us to the painful task of getting dressed. Clara groaned at every move, and I whimpered when I tried to raise my arms. The hard earth under our tarp had ravaged our bodies every bit as much as tumbling down the hill in a runaway truck.

"Auntie, is that my truck, or am I hearing things?" I buckled my sandals and rolled up the tarp.

"I hear it too, and, yes, it's the truck," she said, smoothing down her wrinkled muumuu with both hands. "How do I look?"

"Like a lovely pink-haired lady wearing a wrinkled muumuu."

The engine stopped and a minute later Paul was back with mostly good news. All mechanical parts except the lights were working as far as he could tell, but the bad news included some sizable dents in the body. Paul said it would take a special rig to hoist the truck up to the road.

I made a mental note to call Barry, my insurance guy.

Paul stood on the beach running his big toe through the sand. "I'm sorry, ladies, but I have to leave now. The sun's already up. Here's my phone so you can call for help. Please don't tell them about me."

"Thank you, my dear," Clara said. "If I had a child, I would want him to be like you."

Paul's cheeks blushed.

I walked with him as far as the truck. "I'll see you tonight…."

"Huh? You mean you want to see who picks up the medicine?"

"Yes, I do, because that will be the person who murdered Mac."

"I don't know about that, Josephine, but I need to get home before someone sees me." With long strides, Paul climbed the steep bank like it was a walk in the park and disappeared into the shadows. The forest belonged to him and he belonged to it. Looking at his footprints, I realized he would never be ordinary, average or accepted by the world I lived in. But I felt privileged to know him.

A 911 operator named Michelle responded to my call immediately and asked me to stay on the line. After my brief explanation of deer trouble, she said a responder was on the way and reminded me to stay on the line. With one hand on the phone and one hand free to grab rocks and branches as needed, I slid down to the beach.

"Josephine, are you calling for help?" Clara asked.

I nodded.

The operator asked if we were injured. Were we in a safe place and so on. After all the preliminaries, the woman asked why I hadn't called earlier. My explanation about a lost phone didn't sit well with her, but she didn't hang up. She said a sheriff would arrive in forty minutes.

"Auntie, can you wait forty minutes for help?"

"Certainly, dear, it's lovely here. May I borrow the phone?"

I told the operator I needed to call someone. She finally let me hang up if I promised to call back if we had any more problems.

Clara called Ben, who had been up all night searching the highway with David. She explained about the deer, and that we were fifty or a hundred feet down from the road, approximately five minutes north of Boulder Creek on the Big Basin Highway. Her eyes looked wet, probably because both of us were finally realizing how close we had come to disaster. She ended the call and handed me the phone, wiping her eyes with the back of her hand.

Mom and Dad wouldn't hear from me because they probably didn't know we were missing, so why upset them.

"Auntie, you stay here. I'm going to see if I can make it up to the highway…."

"It won't be easy," she warned.

"Don't worry; I've been doing some hiking around Ben Lomond."

"Good luck, dear."

Just getting back up to the truck was a real "stretch-of-the-legs." Actually, stretching the legs helped my muscles feel better. But the bruises and scrapes would need time to heal. More than once, patches of wild blackberry bushes and poison oak blocked my way, sending me the long way around and up as the embankment became steeper. But the hardest part was pulling myself up, holding onto branches, lifting and placing one foot at a time on the crumbly earth.

Highway sounds were getting louder.

A vehicle rumbled by.

My heart pounded.

Another vehicle came along. It idled several yards above me.

I yelled.

The engine roared and moved away until all was quiet.

A blue jay squawked, leaves rustled in the light breeze and a squirrel watched me from a crook in a tree. For a moment, I wanted to be like Paul—one with the forest. But I snapped out of that thought pretty fast and doubled my determination to beat gravity, one inch at a time.

With small rocks constantly being unearthed and rattling down the hill behind me, and Aunt Clara's voice in my head saying, "Good luck, dear," I barely heard the sound of someone walking on dry leaves. The crunching came closer.

Ten more feet up the bank and I would be standing on good old highway blacktop.

"Hello…help…anyone up there?"

"Is that you, Josie?"

Suddenly my heart leaped. "I'm down here."

"I'm coming. Don't worry," David shouted, peering over the embankment, suddenly catching sight of a disheveled woman clinging to a root. A minute later, he was right above me, holding out his hand. I took it and he pulled me up like I was a stuffed Teddy bear.

Our embrace was short but would stay in my memory forever. As soon as he let go, my body headed for Mother Earth. He caught me before I landed and sat down beside me.

A car whizzed by.

I wept and snuggled while David supported me with his arm.

Three fully uniformed adult bicyclists sped by using the bike lane. A minute later, three more of the same passed by us. A white Ford 150 pulled to the side of the road, and Ben rushed up to us wearing a worried but happy face.

"David, you found your gal, where's mine?"

I pointed down the cliff. "She's waiting for you at the river."

"The river? You gotta be kidding…."

"Not kidding, but don't worry, she's okay."

"Clara told me she was down an embankment, but she didn't say anything about the river." He already had two legs over the edge. His foot slipped. He disappeared from sight as rocks avalanched down the cliff, and then all was quiet.

"Ben?" David shouted, as we peered into the abyss.

"I'll be more careful the rest of the way," Ben shot back, as he climbed over a fallen tree and continued his downhill journey.

A few minutes later, a green and white cruiser pulled to a stop behind Ben's truck. Sergeant Smothers and Deputy Wolf marched single-file up to us, looking at me like I had an ugly three-inch scab on my forehead.

One hand automatically went to my forehead where my fingers found and pulled off a dried slab of barbecue sauce.

Feeling my embarrassment, David tried to help by pulling leaves and twigs from my tangled hair.

"Ms. Stuart, where is your vehicle?" Smothers asked.

I pointed down the bank.

The two deputies walked to the edge and looked down.

"Are you sure it's down there, ma'am?" Officer Wolf said.

"Nobody brought it up, so I think it's still there," I said.

"Is the other victim still down there?" Sergeant Smothers asked.

I nodded. "Her husband went down to get her, but they might need some help."

The men gave each other manly looks, turned back to the cliff and slid the first twenty feet, coming to a jolting stop against a fallen tree, just like Ben.

Half an hour went by. A very large tow truck arrived. The driver stayed busy on his phone while we all waited for Clara and three men to surface. Smothers was the last to make it up to the road, red faced and sucking air. A three-inch scab on his forehead would have been an improvement in his dirty, ragged appearance. He obviously was not "one" with the forest.

Officer Wolf pulled out a notebook and pen. He addressed Clara, "Ma'am, how did the accident happen?"

"A deer jumped…." I said.

"I'll get your version in a minute." He turned back to Clara. "Ma'am, what can you tell me about the accident?"

"I can't tell you much because I didn't see the deer. I think I might have been napping at the time. Josephine was so quick…the deer got away unharmed," she smiled.

"Too bad my truck didn't get off that easy," I mumbled.

When the questions were all answered and the tow truck driver and his helper began their work, Clara and I crawled into the back seat of the Ford 150, David in the passenger seat and Ben in the driver's seat. Ben drove us up the Big Basin Highway, took a left on Tinker and parked in front of Clara's Nest.

We enjoyed a warm welcome from Solow and Sara. Nothing like dog kisses to make me forget my battered and bruised body. Poor Clara looked like she needed more than just dog kisses.

It would have been a nice afternoon for all sorts of things, biking, boating, hiking; but my aunt and I had other plans. We needed rest, but I couldn't rest until I talked to Alicia. I dialed her number from Ben's vintage black telephone that was twice as old as Dad's Buick.

Alicia answered. "Jo, what happened to you…?"

"Hi, Allie. last night on our way to Aunt Clara's, I swerved to miss a deer in the road. My truck went off a cliff, but Aunt Clara and I are fine…just bruised, nothing broken. But we didn't get rescued until this morning and now we're just resting."

"Jo, how do you manage to…oh never mind. I'm so glad you're okay. I knew there must be a good reason keeping you away from work. Kyle and I made some good progress today. You just rest. We can finish what's left tomorrow."

"I'll be there tomorrow, don't worry," I said with more energy than I could spare. As soon as we hung up, I pulled my dead phone from my purse and plugged it into the charger.

Ben announced he would drive David back to his Jeep, which was parked at Daisy's house. But David worried about me and thought I should go home with him. I finally convinced him I would be fine, I just needed a bath and a nap. I told him that the prop painting was almost finished, but I wanted to be there to push it over the finish line.

David relented, saying he would be back Monday afternoon to drive me home from work. He kissed me goodbye and off they went.

Clara sat down on the sofa, her eyes closed, and she was asleep. After a warm bath and a snack from the kitchen, I went down the hall to the guest room and stretched out on the bed. A few hours later, I woke up with a start, checked my watch and thought to myself, "How am I going to get back to Daisy's house without my truck?"

Chapter 26

Sunday afternoon, smoky savory scents drifted through Aunt Clara's house, down the hall and into the guest room where I had slept the afternoon away. I figured catching up on sleep was a good thing since I planned to be on a stakeout half the night.

Clara peeked into my room. "Oh, you're awake. Are you hungry for dinner, dear?"

Solow came out from under the bed, eyes big, tongue hanging.

"Something smells really good," I yawned and stretched. "I was dreaming about my birthday. Allie gave me a beautiful layer cake, and before I could cut into it, Kyle came along and poured barbecue sauce all over it. Even Solow turned it down."

"I hate to tell you this, but Ben's barbecuing. I didn't have the heart to tell him that we ate all the barbecued ribs last night," she laughed. "Actually, my tummy feels a little queasy just thinking about all that sauce."

"I know what you mean," I said. "I just remembered something. Daisy's having a couple of Tabatha's new friends over for dinner tonight, and she asked if I would help her prepare the food. I think she's not used to having company—makes her nervous."

"I wonder…." Clara looked at the ceiling.

"What, Auntie?"

"Maybe Ben could loan you his old farm truck…it's not pretty, but it runs."

"I don't care how it looks…." I said.

Ben came to the open door, peeked in and put his arms around Clara. "Did I hear someone mention my magnificent green pickup?"

"Yes, Lovey, we were discussing your old farm truck. It seems Josephine needs transportation to and from Ben Lomond."

"Okay, Josephine, if you don't mind driving a no-frills old clunker," he laughed. "But seriously, are you feeling up to driving a truck with a manual shift? Let's just say, it doesn't turn on a dime."

"Thank you, Ben. I would love to borrow your truck. I was wondering how I would get around. I'm staying the night with Daisy, but I'll bring the truck back here after work, tomorrow."

I checked my watch. It was almost five-thirty, and Daisy had planned to serve dinner at seven. I slipped my sandals on and followed Ben through the house to the mega-manly barbecue where he took a moment to check on the meat.

Solow checked on the meat as well, hoping some of it would fall his way.

I said goodbye to Clara and climbed into Ben's Ford 150 with Ben at the wheel. Solow crawled under my feet as we careened down the hill to the barn. We clambered out of the truck and walked a short distance to the barn where Ben opened one half of the over-sized double doors, revealing a 1960 Ford 100.

"Just like you said, Ben, old and green. But I think it's cute."

"Cute? Are you calling my work truck, cute?" Ben chuckled. He handed me the key. "I remember the last time I watched you shift gears in a pickup. Try to get the clutch pedal all the way down before you shift."

"I'll do better this time," I promised as I climbed into the cab. Ben hoisted Solow into the passenger seat and the door slammed solidly. The steering wheel seemed so big and the white-knobbed gearshift was about two feet long and mounted to the floor. Just the well-worn bench seat alone was such a novelty. I looked up at the frayed and stained headliner, remembering the clean white headliner in my Dad's old Buick sedan.

That was when the reality of my own smashed up truck hit me like a two-by-four on the head. My Mazda and I had been through so much together. How could I get along without my pickup truck? Any other truck was just a truck.

Moments later, I was able to put sad truck thoughts aside and start the engine with a few turns of the key. The engine roared, sputtered and roared again.

Solow gave me a questioning look.

Ben dodged a puff of smelly black smoke and wished me luck, probably praying I wouldn't hurt his truck.

Underway at last, the old workhorse rumbled down the highway toward Boulder Creek. My hands were so busy steering and shifting that I had no time for anything else.

Solow crawled into a roomy space under the long dashboard.

About four miles short of Boulder Creek, I noticed half a dozen orange cones lining the road and shifted down to second gear. A man wearing an orange vest flagged me to a stop. I pulled up behind a light blue Chevy compact. From my side window, I watched my little red Mazda being secured onto a long trailer attached to a different tow truck than the one I had seen earlier in the day—a bigger truck boasting a king-size winch and pulley system.

A perspiring bearded gentleman left his little blue car and walked up to my window.

Solow gave a quick bark.

"Ms. Stuart, is that your truck?" Archie nodded his head toward the loading process across the street.

"Yep, I don't know how I'll get along without it," I said, feeling a knot in my throat.

"So, you went over the side?" he asked, but before I could answer, he said he had a sweet little pickup for sale at the car lot, and promised me a special low price.

In my mind, I rolled my eyes. "Thanks, but I'm not looking for another truck. Mine just needs some cosmetic help…."

"Yeah, a lot of it," Archie snorted. "Let me get this straight, the truck went over the cliff, you think it still runs and you aren't dead…."

"That's right, and my Aunt survived as well."

"And that would be your Aunt Clara, which explains why you're driving Ben's old truck."

"How do you know all that?"

"It's a small town. I help out at the theater now and then. By the way, your young friend, Albert, gave a very convincing presentation at the water board meeting." He cleared his throat. "I have actually changed my mind on the matter." Archie kicked a pinecone to the side of the road.

"That's wonderful. What happens next?"

"We have to wait for the election in the fall, but I'll put my weight behind a 'no' vote," he said, as if it was a done deal. "Mac and I were pretty close friends until I brought up the dam project. Sure wish I hadn't."

"Then you probably know all about Mac's son living in Minnesota…."

"Uh, sure, he was always bragging about the kid."

"Excuse me, Archie, I need to talk to the tow truck driver." I crossed the two-lane highway as a black sedan heading north was flagged to a stop. Three cars in ten minutes—not exactly a high-traffic road. As I approached the chrome-studded mega-huge tow truck, the driver looked up from his work. "Ma'am?"

"Hi, this is my truck and I need to know where you're taking it."

"They told me you rode this thing down the cliff," he laughed.

"Yeah, thanks to a deer in the road."

"Really?" He cocked his head in disbelief.

"So, where are you taking my truck?" I asked.

"Buena Vista Junk Yard…."

"What? You can't do that…I want you to take it to The Body Shop in Watsonville." I stuck out my chin and gave him my toughest squinty-eyed look.

"Lady, it'll cost a fortune to fix, if it can be fixed. Your insurance will 'total' it for sure."

"I don't care; I love my truck…."

Archie walked up behind me. "Do what the lady says."

"No problem," the man said, as he clamped another chain in place. He climbed into his "over-compensation-truck" and rolled down the highway with Archie following close behind. I tagged along behind the little blue car all the way to Ben Lomond. Archie turned off at Dove Creek. I drove one more block to Daisy's neighborhood, wondering if I would catch Archie in my stakeout since he obviously knew about Mac's so-called son visiting from Minnesota. And if he knew that much, he probably knew about the homemade remedies.

Ben's truck was bigger and wider than my nifty little pickup. I parked as usual along side the road in front of Daisy's place, feeling like the truck was sticking out too far. I shifted into reverse, backed up and tried again. The engine died. I dropped it into neutral and turned the key a few times. The engine roared as the truck belched and black smoke appeared in my rearview mirror. I shifted into reverse and tried again.

"Crack!"

I looked down at Solow. "What was that?" Shoving the shifter into first gear, I pulled the steering wheel to the right a stitch. The motor roared as the truck moved forward a couple of feet. I braked and killed the engine. Feeling exhausted, I watched Daisy open the front door. My arms ached and my left foot felt wobbly from pushing the clutch down so many times. Maybe I wasn't the "pioneer" I thought I was—just a hapless girl after all.

Daisy studied the truck, then walked behind it.

I climbed out of the front seat and met her at the tailgate.

"Maybe that old truck is too big for you," Daisy giggled.

"Oh my gosh, I'm so sorry…." I said, looking at the mailbox lying on the ground with half a post still attached, the other half poking out of the ground like a wounded gopher.

"Never mind that, Josephine, Albert will install a new post. I need your help in the kitchen. Tabatha's friends will be here in half an hour, and the lasagna keeps sliding to one side, and my berry pie over-flowed all over the oven, and everything is such a mess."

Daisy was so frazzled that The Girls forgot about Solow and followed her into the kitchen, probably thinking she might need their help at any moment. Or maybe they just wanted to lick the floor. Her kitchen looked like it had been tossed in the air, sending flour, sugar, berries and tomato sauce everywhere.

"Let's hope they're late," I said, digging into the mess with a wet rag. When all the sweeping and mopping was finished, we concentrated on presentation, trying to make the food look good. I cut burnt stuff off the lasagna and propped it up with toothpicks while Daisy scraped blackened bits of crust off the berry pie.

"Now, show me where your plates, silverware and napkins are"

Daisy bustled around pulling out everything I needed for the table. She even brought out an empty vase and a pair of scissors.

"Daisy, you work on the salad while I pick flowers for the table."

I took the path down to Paul's room but didn't stop there. I rounded the corner of the house and there they were, lovely red geraniums. I cut as many as I thought would fit in the vase and sprinted back to the kitchen.

Daisy looked at me with panic in her eyes. "They're here…."

"It's going to be fun. Just relax."

Wanda and Willow stood at the open front door. Tabatha and her three girlfriends piled out of a red Camaro and burst into the house without ceremony, laughing at teenage silly stuff.

Kit followed the happy teens into the house. "I hope y'all are ready for a night without sleep," she laughed. "These girls are wound!" She turned to leave, but Daisy grabbed her arm.

"Would you like to stay for dinner, Kit?"

"Oh, golly no, I need some peace and quiet," she said and walked out the door. I felt like following her to some place peaceful and quiet. But my plan was to stay the night at Daisy's, no matter what.

Albert came home just in time for dinner. He had spent his day working on his friend's car. Everyone waited patiently for him, as he scrubbed oil and grease off his hands and fingernails. Finally he came to the table, and we started off with our individual salads and ended with berry pie and ice cream. Ice cream was the perfect topping for a satisfactory meal.

The four teenage girls couldn't have cared less about the food. They talked and giggled their way through the meal and dessert. From there they moved into the living room for a movie.

Albert didn't look interested and went to his room.

Daisy and I stayed in our chairs at the table, each of us trying to working up enough energy to clean the dishes and the kitchen.

"Josephine, would you mind taking leftovers down to Paul?"

"Not at all."

"If he's not there, just place everything in the wood box."

"Have you seen him today?"

"No, not today." She smiled bravely.

Chapter 27

While Tab and her three girlfriends watched a movie on TV in Daisy's living room, I ducked out the sliding glass doors, crossed the deck and padded down steep wooden stairs carrying a foil-covered platter of food for Paul. At the bottom of the stairs, it was just one right turn and ten feet up the path to his door. I placed the platter on top of the wood box and tried the door. It was locked. I knocked. No sound from inside. Giving up, I carefully placed the platter in the empty wood box and closed the lid, deciding to check on the box later. I hoped Paul would show up soon.

Crickets sang their songs and an almost full moon rose up over the treetops. The sky was deep purple—going black—and the stars were coming out to play. I was comfortable wearing my shorts, t-shirt and sandals, but realized I would need to borrow a jacket or a blanket to keep warm in the wee hours. I planned to begin my stakeout at midnight, unless Paul came home sooner.

I checked my watch. Still three long hours until I would be hiding behind the rhododendron bush, armed with a flashlight and pepper spray. All the way up the path to the front door, I heard four teenage girls shrieking and laughing like hyenas at a food-fest. It wasn't the movie entertaining them. They only needed each other to keep the good times rolling.

I found Daisy and Al at the kitchen table playing cards. Solow and The Girls rested under the table, two rooms away from the teenagers.

"Josephine, is Paul in his room?" Daisy asked.

"No, not yet. What game are you two playing?"

"We're playing twenty-one," Albert said. "My dad was a dealer in Vegas when he was young. He taught Tab and me all kinds of card tricks."

"That's great, Al. Do you have room for me?"

"Have a seat, Josephine," Daisy said, "I would have invited you to play cards sooner but I thought you were going home."

"Actually, I'm too tired and sleepy to drive home. I was hoping I could share the couch with The Girls tonight."

"Of course, my dear, but I doubt any of us will get much sleep tonight," Daisy lamented.

"I can sleep through anything," Al said, showing us his two kings and one ace, as he raked in all four pennies with glee.

"Al, deal me in," I said, "and by the way, can you remember who was at the theater the day Mac went missing?"

"Ah, let me think. I walked down there around noon with…" he hesitated, and looked at Daisy for a moment. She said nothing. He continued, "Yeah, it was just before lunch and Daisy brought a sandwich for Mac and Tab was carrying a bag of homemade peanut butter cookies for everyone. We looked all around but we never found Uncle Mac. As you know, we tried again that evening."

"Who else was there?"

Daisy spoke up, "I remember going to the back room with Tabatha and The Girls. Kate and Clara were back there singing to some country song. Willow poked my arm, letting me know that the baby was under the steps—that's what she's trained to do."

"Then what happened?" I asked.

"Kate immediately pulled Gypsy out from under the staircase…."

"And then?"

"Well, let's see. I remember Tab offering the ladies some cookies."

"Al, were you in the back room?"

Al shook his head. "No."

"Daisy, was the door to the attic open or closed?"

"Oh dear, I didn't even notice. I just called Wanda down from the landing, and I remember Frank searching for his beer opener by the sink and I wondered why the music was so loud. That was when Sara pushed her way through the crowd, straight to Tabatha's bag of cookies. Of course, your aunt was there quick as a whistle, but it was too late," Daisy giggled.

"Anyone else in the room?"

"Janinne grabbed a broom and swept up the crumbs—that's all that was left after three dogs and a baby gobbled up the cookies. It was so hot back there, I had to leave. But I couldn't leave without The Girls. I plopped down on a bench and The Girls were there at my side in an instant, bless their hearts."

"Then what happened?"

Daisy thought for a moment. "Well, I couldn't wait to get away from the heat and the noise. I walked to the entrance door for some fresh air. About one minute later, everyone decided they needed a break and we all went to lunch in the park." Daisy looked at me with sad eyes. "I ate Mac's tuna sandwich. What kind of wife does that?"

Al reached over and touched her shoulder. "You were a good wife," he said, with no trace of doubt in his voice.

"Hey, look at this," I laughed, placing my cards on the table face up. "Four, five and six of hearts."

"Wrong game," Al quipped. "Besides, Daisy's ace and two queens have you beat." He slapped his cards on the table: two sevens and a king adding up to twenty-four when twenty-one was the limit.

"Sorry old boy, you can't win them all," I laughed.

"Josephine," Daisy said, "I just remembered something. Archie was there too, snooping around the back room for a flashlight he said he'd left by the sink."

"Did he find it?"

"I don't know," Daisy said. "Archie was still looking around the back room when I left to get some fresh air. He was red-faced and sweating like Frank—but Frank always sweats, even when it's cold outside."

"Was George there?"

"He was in the alley," Al said. "He was watching Kit draw a palm tree on some plywood. He started to cut it out with a jigsaw, and that's when she left the building." He folded his hand: a king, a queen and a nine, and excused himself from the table explaining that he had go to work early the next morning.

When I heard Albert's door close, I asked Daisy about the uncomfortable chewing out Mac had given Al in front of everyone at the theater. Daisy said that Mac and Al had gone down to the theater around nine, Friday morning. Daisy said she didn't know about the scolding. All she knew was that Al had walked home alone an hour later. A couple of hours after that, Tabatha, Albert and The Girls had walked Daisy into town for her first ever visit to the Ben Lomond Theater.

"Daisy, did you hear something outside?" I asked.

She yawned. "I can't hear a thing over those crazy teenage girls in the living room. I didn't know *Star Wars* was such a funny film—or do they just laugh at nothing in particular?"

"They are definitely having a good time," I said.

"Goodnight, Josephine, I don't know if I'll be able to sleep tonight, but I'm going to go lie down." She headed down the hall to her room and I went in the other direction, out the kitchen sliding glass doors, across the deck and down the stairs to Paul's room.

I tapped lightly on his door. It opened.

"Josephine, what are you doing here?" Paul stepped back, letting me walk inside. The room smelled like a musty potpourri of herbs, spices and lasagna. As soon as my eyes adjusted to the dim light, I spied the lasagna platter on his desktop. Not a crumb of food remained. He sat down on the edge of his bed.

"Did you enjoy your dinner?"

He nodded. "What are you doing here?"

"I'm here to see who picks up the meds…."

"She picked them up about half an hour ago…."

"What?" I leaped out of the chair and stared at Paul. "She, who? Who picked up the medicine? I wanted to be here…." I stammered.

"Calm down, Josephine. Kit told me she's desperate to cure George's mother's cancer. She thinks the illness is getting in the way of their romance. It seems she might be pregnant and wants to get married as soon as possible."

"How did she know about you and your medicines?"

"Because Mac did some bragging about a supposed son living out of state. Kit asked Tabatha a few questions and then Daisy. Poor Daisy got all flustered and told Kit there were no children living inside the house except Albert and Tabatha. But the way she said it, Kit was curious. She came back and prowled around the property one night and found my room on her own. She slipped the notes under the door."

"Kit must have been busy, coming and going…."

"Yeah, searched my files on one of those visits, but tonight she apologized for all the things she did."

"Did she pay you for the medicine?"

"She tried to. I told her it was a wedding present," he chuckled.

"And she sat there and told you she was pregnant? Probably looking for sympathy," I growled.

"She didn't tell me…I just sense things," he smiled. "Kit didn't mean any harm, but she thought that threatening to harm Tabatha would insure cooperation from me."

"Have there been any more notes under the door?"

"No," he grinned. "Yesterday, Kit asked Al to get my email address. He had no idea what was going on, but did what he was told and got the address from Daisy. Of course she was happy to give it, thinking Al wanted to chat with me so we could be friends."

"Are you and Al getting along…?"

"Al and I are still getting to know each other. I think we will be very good friends someday," Paul said, thoughtfully. "And Tabatha and I are already texting each other."

"Are you texting Kit?"

"Yes, but just to arrange the meeting we had tonight. She explained that she meant no harm to Tab or anyone else."

"I hope she means what she says," I said under my breath.

Paul rolled his eyes—probably for the first time in his life, and hinted to me that I should have more faith in people. Maybe we both needed more of that. I told Paul I would try not to judge people in the future, if he promised not be so hard on himself.

We said goodnight, and I trotted upstairs to the noisiest sleepover in town. Even The Girls looked uncomfortable, pacing from room to room looking for quiet sanity.

I checked my watch. It was eleven-thirty. I could drive forty miles to my house or put up with the noise and try to sleep on Daisy's couch. It was a no-brainer. But before I went inside, I stood in the moonlight breathing deeply, counting stars. Life was good, except for one nagging problem: who killed Mac? I had put so much effort into finding the murderer and had nothing to show for it. Like Paul said, I shouldn't judge people harshly. Archie had turned out to be a nice guy with good intentions, George just wanted to help his mother get well, and Kit wanted to get married and raise a family.

I had run out of possibilities, and I still loathed the idea of someone getting away with murder.

Chapter 28

Early Monday morning I found myself on Daisy's couch, curled into a ball because Solow needed his room too. My mood was pretty much the same as it had been the night before—rotten. Feelings of disappointment and failure gripped me and wouldn't let go. I had failed miserably. No one had been blamed for Mac's murder, no murderer languished in a jail cell and justice had not been served.

On the bright side, the props looked good and we only had a few small details left to paint. Alicia and I would complete the finishing touches, and we would have the rest of the day off.

Tabatha bounced into the room full of teenage energy.

"Good morning, Josephine."

"Good morning, Tab, where are your friends?"

"In my room. I guess they need more sleep than I do," she laughed.

"So what do you think of Kit?" I asked.

"She's nice, once you get to know her. Shall I put the coffee on for you?"

I nodded. "You're a doll. Will you be at the theater today?"

"Oh sure, more songs to practice." She grinned ear-to-ear. "Thursday is our first show." Tab headed for the kitchen and The Girls trotted along behind her, tails raised to the "happy" position. From the couch, I heard kibble clinking into stainless steel bowls and clickity-click basset toenails running urgently across hardwood flooring. Solow had never missed a meal in his life, and he wasn't about to start.

Passing all three bedrooms on my way to the shower, I noticed Daisy was asleep in her bed, Tabatha's three friends were still asleep in sleeping bags on the floor and Al's bed was empty.

Living in a valley with high mountains to the East and mountains to the West offered more dark time, conducive to good sleep. Even though the air was already warming and the sky was light blue, the mid-summer sun would not reveal itself until eight in the morning and would disappear around four in the afternoon.

The smell of bacon frying was our call to breakfast. Tabatha's friends and Daisy and I congregated at the kitchen table to watch the making of scrambled eggs, bacon and toast. Tab whipped around the kitchen like someone who had learned to cook out of necessity long before she came to live with her Aunt Daisy.

The teenagers watched Tab and complimented her on her cooking. I wondered if these girls could understand and appreciate a girl so gifted. If the girls had integrity, they would forgive Tab for being so bright and talented. Just like water finding its own level, I was sure she would always find worthy friends.

I turned to Daisy, "I suppose Al is already at work…."

She giggled. "He's an official stagehand at the theater. George is showing him how to move the props and later Janinne will tell him when to move them. They have three days to practice before the show starts."

"I'm glad to see Al getting involved," I said, passing a platter of crispy bacon to the girl on my right.

Solow barked at the front door.

I stood up, walked into the living room and peeked out the door. Kit stood there in the warm morning air flicking pine needles off her lacy white blouse. Living in the forest was like that.

"Hi, Josephine, are the girls ready to go?"

"So soon?"

"I promised to take them to the beach in Santa Cruz. We're going to do an 'all-girls day' since the fog finally left the coast."

"Wow, Kit, that sounds wonderful…and I must say, you look great…." I noticed the 'rock' was on her ring finger again.

She smiled. "Thanks, I feel wonderful."

"Hormones…."

"Huh? Yeah, maybe." Kit cocked her head to one side. I wondered if she knew what I knew and Paul knew. If she didn't, she would soon enough. If she did know, maybe she wondered how I knew. But that was a question for another day.

As soon as Kit drove away with the three teens giggling over anything and everything, Tab, Solow and I hoofed it down to the theater. It was nine o'clock and the sun had begun to show its face. The still morning air had already lost its freshness as the temperature rose.

Volunteer workers and young actors stood three-deep on the sidewalk outside the theater. A new level of excitement permeated the air. Just three days to show time. Janinne and Kate stood at the curb assigning each child a particular teacher and an allotted space in the building. Organizing over seventy children took skill and courage. By the time I climbed my assigned ladder, the kids were calmly practicing their numbers. Oh to be young and able to pick up dance moves so easily.

Aunt Clara had a group of little pirates singing and dancing around a pretend fire—a chair with a red tablecloth draped over it. Close by was a team of little

Indians and another fake fire. Eventually all the boys merged together for a final song.

Gypsy had crawled under one of the fake fires. She peek-a-booed the kids as they whooped it up, round and round.

A dozen teenage mermaids sang and danced along the North wall, and a teenage boy ran through his crocodile dance routine.

Solow found a safe spot under the sink in the back room.

Sara stretched out on the concrete floor nearby.

Alicia arrived and scampered up her ladder. We worked just a few feet from each other. But with all the music, singing and dancing, we could not talk to each other and be heard. As a result, the work went quickly and by twelve, we were finished with our painting except for a few minor touchups. I stood back and looked at all the work we had done.

"Jo, don't tell me we missed something," Alicia said, her purse already hooked over her shoulder.

"No, not really. I was just thinking, what if we glued a piece of canvas onto the ship—the biggest sail? I think it would be even more of a three-dimensional look…."

"It might work, but where would you get the material?" she asked.

"Don't worry, Allie, I know where to find all kinds of material. You go ahead and buy your sandwich and one for me. I'll pay you when I get to the park."

She turned and followed the last group of children out the door.

I put Alicia's brushes and mine in a bucket of water beside the sink. Solow and Sara had already left for the park, happy to be with the crowd and near food. That left me. The building was so quiet it seemed spooky. I shivered, even though it was ninety-eight degrees in the back room. As I climbed the stairs, the heat intensified. Sweat ran down my spine. I wiped my brow, and ignored rumors of a ghost living in the building.

Entering the attic was like entering a giant furnace. I told myself I must be quick, find the fabric and leave. As I pawed over a pile of fabric remnants, I thought I heard something or someone in the back room. I walked to the door and was surprised to see The Girls galloping up the steps. They pushed past me and sniffed the stuffed animals and a fake potted geranium.

A high-pitched whistle spat twice.

The Girls immediately turned and ran out the door. The last dog out bumped the door shut. Faintly, I heard Daisy calling her dogs and then all was quiet.

Just when I thought I couldn't take another minute of hot stuffy air, I found the perfect piece of white canvas. I would cut it to the right size and shape and glue it to the ship. I was so excited.

Ready to leave, I turned the doorknob and pushed on the door. At first I thought the door was stuck or jammed. But even after throwing my weight at it, the door did not budge.

Kicking and screaming didn't help my predicament because everyone was on a lunch break across the street. I looked around for a heavy, sharp object—anything that would break the door down. Everything I saw was either stuffed, or soft, or made out of cardboard or glass. My head hurt and salty sweat stung my eyes. Too bad old doors were so solidly built.

My heart pounded in my ears as I listened to an empty theater.

Minutes ticked by. I knew I had to get out soon or I would be the next fatality. Front page *Sentinel*: "Another Victim of Stupidity."

The stuffed animals glared at me as if to say, "What's your problem?" The gorilla looked especially critical. I felt like punching him one minute, and the next I was squeezing his big fury body, eyes closed, crying all over his plastic face.

Still holding the gorilla, I opened my eyes and saw a piece of a door I had seen once before. Mr. Gorilla was immediately tossed aside. Other stuffies landed in a pile on the floor. I sucked air like a vacuum cleaner, as I worked to expose two hinges and a doorknob on a very special little door.

Suddenly, I noticed I wasn't sweating anymore and the room was looking like a Santa Cruz beach when the fog rolls in. Taking that as a bad sign, I went full-throttle, yanking the doorknob off its rusty stem. Falling backward onto a pile of stuffed animals wasn't so bad; it was the thought of never seeing David again that hurt. How would Solow survive without me? And Mom and Dad would be devastated.

Grabbing the newly exposed doorknob shaft, I turned it with pinched fingers and threw my body weight against the door. The door opened quicker than expected. Suddenly I found myself sprawled out on the metal mesh floor of a catwalk, two-feet wide with four-foot-high metal railings running east to west. The theater's peaked roof ran in the same direction six feet overhead. I rose up on one knee, grabbed a metal post and pulled myself up to a precarious standing-swaying position.

Looking down about twenty feet to the stage area, nothing looked real. Tables, chairs and props swam in circles. I blinked and squinted, but the blur didn't go away. Even with all the hot air rising to the rafters, the temperature was still about five degrees lower than inside the attic. Maybe I would survive after all.

At the end of the catwalk, about forty feet ahead, was a metal door. Focusing on the door was easy, getting there took some hard work since my balance was missing and the door danced to the right, swam to the left and floated up out of sight. Breathing hard, I finally stood close enough to reach out and try the doorknob.

"Aacckk!" I screamed just before I heard footsteps down below.

"Who's up there? Is that you, Jo?" Alicia shouted. She was the first to enter the building from lunch break. A blur of voices and footsteps followed her inside.

"Allie, help…help, I'm up here, and I'm going to pass out."

"Okay, I see you. Is that door locked?" She didn't wait for an answer, she just ran to the North wall, made a left and scrambled up the steep stairs leading to a little office adjacent to the lighting station.

With both armpits draped over the railing and head facing the floor, I heard the squeak of a door opening, looked up and saw Alicia's frightened face. Quickly, silently, she hooked my arm over her shoulder while hers wrapped around my lower back. She walked me into a small office featuring two desks and three chairs, all swimming right and left. Alicia poured me into one of the chairs and felt my forehead.

"Okay, Jo, stay there a minute." She poked her head out the door and shouted to people filing through the front door. Clara was one of those people.

Moments later, we heard Aunt Clara huffing and puffing up the steps, Sara right behind her. The other office door burst open and my overwrought auntie came to me in a dither, wanting to know why my face was so red.

Alicia explained, "I found Jo on the catwalk." She pointed to the open door.

The noise level increased as people poured into the building from the park. Loud music filled the air. The children began singing the first song in the "Penny Pamilton" play.

Alicia ran downstairs and a few minutes later was back with a bottle of water and a stack of wet paper towels. By the time she and Clara doused me with cold water and brought my temperature down to normal, the children were singing the farewell song, the last song of the play.

As my mind slowly became useable, questions popped into my head. I remembered seeing The Girls in the attic, and someone blew a whistle and the dogs left. And the door was shut. And locked!

"Allie, Aunt Clara, do you know who brought The Girls down to the theater today?"

"Daisy…." Alicia said.

"And Albert…." Clara said.

"Who blew the whistle?"

Clara looked up at the ceiling. "I noticed a string with a whistle on it around Al's neck."

"I saw it too," Alicia said. "Why do you ask?"

"I have a theory. Let's go check out the attic." My heart did an extra beat. The attic was the last place I wanted to be.

Clara and Alicia looked at each other and finally agreed to go with me. The theater was nearly empty at that point in time. We walked slowly, as I had not regained my full strength yet, and my head pounded with a major headache.

"Allie, you go up to the landing and slam the door."

"Okay, I'm up here but the door is locked."

"Unlock it," I directed, "then open it and slam it shut."

Alicia flipped the latch up to one side, opened the door and then slammed it shut. "Oh, look at that! The lock fell into place by itself," she said. "Someone needs to toss this old lock. What's it good for anyway?"

"Josephine, dear, who slammed the door while you were inside?"

Suddenly everything made sense to me. The curtains of misinformation and suspicion parted. "Auntie, it's not a 'who.' It was a dog."

Clara's jaw dropped. "But that's impossible…."

"Not really. I had a little visit from The Girls while I was in the attic. I remember hearing a whistle, the dogs suddenly left the room and the door slammed shut behind them." I began laughing. I couldn't stop laughing. There was no murderer, no fiendish plot, no one to bring to justice. And that felt wonderful. Paul was right, I should have more faith in people. I vowed to give it my best shot.

Epilogue

Two days after watching the fabulous Penny Pamilton play, David and I caught a plane to Hawaii for a little R & R. It was his birthday present to me: a whole three weeks of bliss. While we were gone, Solow stayed with the Quintanas, indulging in his own Tansey bliss.

When we came home, my sweet little truck looked like new and the insurance company had covered seventy-five percent of the cost.

Tabatha and Albert thrived in the small-town atmosphere of Ben Lomond, and Daisy was always there to reinforce their good manners, attitudes and education.

George and Kit married, a baby boy was born, and George's mother miraculously recovered her health. She met Lucky, and another forever match was made.

Archie continued to watch over Park Theater, sometimes entering the building from the stairs he had installed in the basement especially for those times when he misplaced the entrance key.

I kept in touch with Daisy. She reported that Paul spent most of his time in the mountains remodeling the garden shed and growing medicinal plants. He visited Daisy and his cousins at least once a week.

Paul and Professor George Hathaway began working on a formula to reverse schizophrenia. Inch-by-inch, Paul was moving into the big world. He could count his friends on seven fingers, but I heard a rumor that he had met a very tall girl who lived alone in the mountains.

Rumors are just that, rumors. But dreams can come true.

THE END

ABOUT THE AUTHOR

Author, Joyce Oroz, says she is having more fun than ever before as she sends Josephine into an imperfect world to find justice for her friends. Oroz writes her Josephine Stuart Mystery series, enjoys her family and friends and recently found time to illustrate a bi-lingual children's book called Sammy the Dump Truck. If you would like to comment on a book, her email address is….joyceoroz@sbcglobal.net

76438236R00140

Made in the USA
Columbia, SC
04 September 2017